"Sophy, why did you agree to marry me?"

Jon continued before Sophy could answer. "I know you care deeply for the children, but you're a very attractive woman, and there are men who would want to share a far more intimate relationship with you than the one I'm offering."

Sophy felt embarrassed and uncomfortable. "I don't want that kind of relationship."

"I see. Having suffered the pangs of love once and been hurt by it, you have no wish to risk yourself with such an emotion again, is that it?"

"Yes, that is exactly what I mean."

But it wasn't because she was frightened of loving that she'd agreed to marry Jon. It was just simpler to let him believe that than to tell him the truth.

PENNY JORDAN was constantly in trouble in school because of her inability to stop daydreaming—especially during French lessons. In her teens she was an avid romance reader, although it didn't occur to her to try writing one herself until she was older. "My first half-dozen attempts ended up ingloriously," she remembers, "but I persevered, and one manuscript was finished." She plucked up the courage to send it to a publisher, convinced her book would be rejected. It wasn't—and the rest is history! Penny is married and lives in Cheshire.

Books by Penny Jordan

These books may be available at your local bookseller.

Don't miss any of our special offers. Write to us at the following address for information on our newest releases.

Harlequin Reader Service
901 Fuhrmann Blvd., P.O. Box 1397, Buffalo, NY 14240
Canadian address: P.O. Box 603,
Fort Erie, Ont. L2A 9Z9

PENNY JORDAN

capable of feeling

Harlequin Books

TORONTO • NEW YORK • LONDON
AMSTERDAM • PARIS • SYDNEY • HAMBURG
STOCKHOLM • ATHENS • TOKYO • MILAN

Harlequin Presents first edition November 1986
ISBN 0-373-10931-8

Original hardcover edition published in 1986
by Mills & Boon Limited

CHAPTER ONE

'DARLING, I do hope you're going to wear something a little more attractive than that for dinner. You know we've got the Bensons coming and he *is* one of your father's best clients. Chris is back by the way.'

Sophy had only been listening to her mother with half her attention, too overwhelmed by the familiar sense of depression, which inevitably overcame her when she had to spend longer than an hour in the latter's company, to resist the tidal flood of maternal criticism but the moment she heard Chris Benson's name mentioned she tensed.

They were sitting in the garden on the small patio in front of the immaculately manicured lawns and rosebeds. The garden was her father's pride and joy but to Sophie it represented everything about her parents and their life-style that had always heightened for her the differences between them. In her parents' lives everything must be neat and orderly, conforming to a set middle-class pattern of respectability.

She had spent all her childhood and teenage years in this large comfortable house in its West Suffolk village and all that time she had felt like an ungainly cuckoo in the nest of two neat, tiny wrens.

She didn't even look like her parents; her mother was five-foot-three with immaculate, still blonde, hair and a plumply corseted figure, her father somewhat taller, but much in the same mould; a country solicitor, who had once been in the army and who still ran his life on the orderly lines he had learned in that institution.

It was not that her parents didn't love her, or weren't kind, genuinely caring people. It was just that she was alien to them and them to her.

Her height, the ungainly length of her legs and arms, the wild mane of her dark, chestnut hair and the high cheekboned, oval face with its slightly tilting gold eyes; these were not things she had inherited from her parents, and she knew that her mother in particular had always privately mourned the fact that her daughter was not like herself, another peaches and cream English rose.

Instead, her physical characteristics had come to her from the half American, half Spanish beauty her great-grandfather had married in South America and brought home. Originally the Marley family had come from Bristol. They had been merchants there for over a century, owning a small fleet of ships and her great-grandfather had been the captain of one of these.

All that had been destroyed by the First World War, which had destroyed so many of the small shipping companies and Sophie knew that her parents felt uneasy by this constant reminder of other times in the shape and physical appearance of their only child.

Her mother had done her best ... refusing to see that her tall, ungainly daughter did not look her best in pretty embroidered dresses with frills and bows.

She had disappointed her mother, Sophy knew that. Sybil Rainer had been married at nineteen, a mother at twenty-one and that was a pattern she would have liked to have seen repeated in her daughter. Once too she . . .

'Of course, Chris is married now . . .'

Her mind froze, distantly registering the hint of reproach in her mother's voice. 'There was a time when I thought that you and he . . .' her voice trailed away and Sophy let it, closing her eyes tightly, thinking bitterly that once she too had thought that she and Chris would marry. Chris's father was a wealthy stockbroker and she had known him all through her teens, worshipping his son in the way that teenage girls are wont to do.

She had never dreamed Chris might actually notice her as anything other than the daughter of one of his father's oldest friends. The year he came down from university, when she herself was just finishing her 'A' levels, he had come home.

They had met at the tennis club. Sophy had just been finishing a match. Tennis was one of the few things she excelled at; she had the body and the strength for it and, she realised with wry hindsight, he could hardly have seen her in a more flattering setting.

He had asked her out; she had been over-whelmed with excitement . . . and so it had started.

Her mouth twisted bitterly. It was not how it had started that she was thinking of now, but how it had finished.

It hadn't taken her long to fall in love—she was literally starving for attention . . . for someone of her own and she had been all too ridiculously easy a conquest for him. Of course she had demurred when he told her he wanted to make love to her but she had also been thrilled that he could want her so much. Seeing no beauty or desirability in her own appearance, she could not understand how anyone else could either.

She had thought he loved her. She had wanted to believe it. She had thought he intended to marry her. God, how ridiculous and farcical it all seemed now.

Inevitably she had let him make love to her, one hot summer night at the end of August when they were alone in his parents' house . . . and that night had shattered her rosy dreams completely.

Even now she could remember his acid words of invective when he realised that she was not enjoying his lovemaking, his criticisms of her as a woman, his disgust in her inability to respond to him.

Frightened by the change in him, her body still torn by the pain of his possession she had sought to placate him offering uncertainly, 'But it will get better when we are married . . .'

'Married!' He had withdrawn completely from her, staring at her with narrowed eyes. 'What the hell are you talking about? I wouldn't marry you if you were the last woman on earth, darling,' he had drawled tauntingly. 'When I get married it will be to a woman who knows what it means to be a woman . . . not a frigid little girl. You'll never get married, Sophy,' he had told her cruelly. 'No man will ever want to marry a woman like you.'

Looking back, she was lucky to have come out of the escapade with nothing worse than a badly bruised body and ego, Sophy told herself. It could have been so much worse. She could have been pregnant . . . pregnant and unmarried.

'Darling, you aren't listening to a word I'm

saying,' her mother complained a little petulantly, 'and why do you scrape your hair back like that? It's so pretty.'

'It's also heavy, Mother . . . and today it's very hot.' She said it patiently, forcing a placatory smile.

'I wish you'd have it properly styled, darling . . . and get some new clothes. Those awful jeans you're wearing . . .'

Sighing faintly, Sophy put down her book. If only her mother could understand that she could not be what she wanted her to be. If only . . .

'I've told Brenda to bring Chris and his wife round to see us. She's a lovely girl, Brenda was saying. An American . . . they got married last year while we were away on that cruise.' She looked across at her daughter. 'It's time you were thinking of settling down, darling, after all *you* are twenty-six . . .'

So she was, and wouldn't Chris just crow to know that his cruel prediction all those years ago had proved so correct.

Not that she wanted to get married. She moved restlessly in her deck chair, unwanted images flashing through her mind . . . pictures of the men she had dated over the years, and the look on their faces when she turned cold and unresponsive in their arms. She had never totally been able to overcome the fears Chris had instilled in her—not of the physical reality of male possession, but of her own inability to respond to him . . . her own innate sexual coldness. Well it was something no other man was ever going to find out about her. It was her own private burden and she was going to carry it alone.

No male possession meant no children, though. Sighing once again, she opened her eyes and stared unseeingly at her father's neat flower border. Just when she had first felt this fierce need to have children of her own she wasn't quite sure but lately she was rarely unaware of it. She very much wanted children . . . a family of her own. But she wasn't going to get them, as Chris had so rightly taunted her. No man was going to want a woman who was physically incapable of responding to him sexually.

The sharp ring of the telephone bell on the wall outside the house cut through her despondent thoughts.

Her mother got up and hurried into the house via the french windows. Several seconds later she reappeared, beckoning Sophy, a frown marring her forehead.

'It's Jonathan,' she told Sophy peevishly. 'Why on earth does he need to ring you at weekends?'

Jonathan Phillips was her boss. Sophy had been working for him for two years. She'd first met him at a party thrown by a mutual acquaintance to which she had gone in a mood of bitter introspection having finally come to the realisation that the happiness and fulfilment of marriage and children would never be hers. She had also been well on her way to getting drunk. She had bumped into him on her way to get herself yet another glass of wine, the totally unexpected impediment of a solidly muscled chest knocking her completely off balance.

Jonathan had grasped her awkwardly round the waist looking at her through his glasses with eyes that registered his discomfort and shock at finding her in his arms.

She had pulled away and he had released her immediately, looking very relieved to do so. She would have walked away and that would have been that if she had not suddenly betrayed her half inebriated state by teetering uncertainly on her high heels.

It was then that Jon had taken charge, dragging her outside into the fresh air, procuring from somewhere a cup of black coffee. Both were acts which, now that she knew him better, were so alien to his normal vague, muddledly hopeless inability to organise anything, that they still had the power to surprise her slightly.

They had talked. She had learned that he was a computer consultant working from an office in Cambridge; that he had his orphaned niece and nephew in his care and that he was the mildest and most unaggressive man she had ever come across.

She, in turn, had told him about her languages degree—gained much to the disapproval of her mother, who still believed that a young woman had no need to earn her own living but should simply use her time to find herself a suitable husband—her secretarial abilities, and the dull job she had working in her father's office.

She had eventually sobered up enough to drive home and by the end of the next week she had forgotten Jonathan completely.

His letter to her offering her a job as his assistant had come totally out of the blue but, after discussing it with him, she had realised that here was the chance she needed so desperately to get herself out of the rut her life had become.

It was then that she realised that Jonathan was one of that elite band of graduates who had emerged from Cambridge in the late 'sixties and early 'seventies, fired by enthusiasm for the new computer age about to dawn, and that Jonathan was a world-renowned expert in his field.

Against her mother's wishes she had accepted the job and on the strength of the generous salary he paid her she had found herself a pleasant flat in Cambridge.

She went into the hall and took the receiver from her mother, who moved away but not out of earshot. Her mother disapproved of Jonathan. Tall, and untidy with a shock of dark hair and mild, dark blue eyes which were always hidden behind the glasses he needed to wear, he was not like the bright, socially adept sons of her friends. Jonathan never indulged in social chit-chat—he didn't know how to. He was vague and slightly clumsy, often giving the impression that he lived almost exclusively in a world of his own. Which in many ways he did, Sophy reflected, speaking his name into the receiver.

'Ah, Sophy . . . thank goodness you're there. It's Louise . . . the children's nanny. She's left . . . and I have to fly to Brussels in the morning. Would you . . .?'

'I'll be there just as soon as I can,' Sophy promised with alacrity, mentally sending a prayer of thanks up to her guardian angel.

Now she had a valid excuse for missing tonight's dinner party and inevitable conversation about Chris.

'What did he want?' her mother questioned as Sophy replaced the receiver.

'Louise, the nanny, has left. He wants me to look after the children for him, until he comes back from Brussels on Wednesday.'

'But you're his secretary,' her mother expostulated. 'He has no right to ring you here at weekends. You're far too soft with him, Sophy. He's only himself to blame ... I've never met a more disorganised man. What he needs isn't a secretary, it's a wife ... and what you need is a husband and children of your own,' she added bitterly. 'You're getting far too attached to those children ... you know that, don't you?'

Mentally acknowledging that her mother was more astute than she had thought, Sophy gave her a brief smile. 'I like them, yes,' she admitted evenly, 'and Jon is my boss. I can hardly refuse his request you know Mother.'

'Of course you can. I wish you weren't working for the man. I don't like him. Why on earth doesn't he do something about himself? He ought to tidy himself up a bit, buy some new clothes ...'

Sophy hid a smile. 'Because those sort of things aren't important to him, mother.'

'But they should be important. Appearance *is* important.'

Maybe for more ordinary mortals, Sophy reflected as she went upstairs to re-pack the weekend bag she had brought with her when she had come home, but the rules that governed ordinary people did not apply to near geniuses and that was what Jon was. He was so involved with his computers that she doubted he was aware of anything else.

At thirty-four he epitomised the caricature of a slightly eccentric, confirmed bachelor totally involved in his work and oblivious to anything else.

Except the children. He was very caring and aware where they were concerned.

As she went back downstairs with her case she frowned slightly. Louise would be the third nanny he had lost in the two years she had worked with him and she was at a loss to understand why. The children were a lovable pair. David, ten, and Alexandra, eight, were lively, it was true, but intelligent and very giving. The house Jonathan lived in had been bought by him when his brother and sister-in-law had died, and was a comfortable, if somewhat rambling, Victorian building on the outskirts of a small Fen village. It had a large garden, which was rather inadequately cared for by an ancient Fensman and the housework was done by a woman who came in from the village to clean twice a week. Jonathan was not an interfering or difficult man to work for.

'You're going then!'

Her mother made it sound as though she was leaving for good.

'I'll try and get down the weekend after next,' she promised, aiming a kiss somewhere in the direction of her mother's cheek and jumping into her newly acquired Metro.

Leaving the house behind her was like shedding an unwanted burden, she thought guiltily as she drove through the village and headed in the direction of Cambridge. It wasn't her parents' fault there was this chasm between them, this inability to communicate on all but the most mundane levels. She loved them, of course, and knew that they loved her . . . but there was no real understanding between them. She felt more at ease and comfortable with Jonathan, more at home in his home than she had ever felt in her own.

Of course it was impossible to imagine anyone

not getting on with him. He could be exasperating, it was true, with his vagueness and his inability to live in any sort of order but he had a wry sense of humour ... a placid nature ... well at least almost. There had been one or two occasions on which she had thought she had seen a gleam of something unexpected in his eyes. Best of all, he treated her as an equal in all respects. He never enquired into her personal life, although they often spent the evening talking when she was down at his home—which was quite often because, although he had an office in Cambridge, there were times when he was called away unexpectedly and he would summon Sophy to his side to find the papers he was always losing and to generally ensure that he was travelling to his destination with all that he would require.

It was through these visits that she had got to know the children, often staying overnight, and this was not the first time she had received a frantic telephone call from Jonathan informing her of some domestic crisis.

Her mother was right, she thought wryly, what he needed was a wife but she could not see him marrying. Jonathan liked the life he had and he appeared to be one of that rare breed of people who seemed to have no perceptible sexual drive at all. His behaviour towards her for instance was totally sexless, as it seemed to be to the whole of her sex—and his own; there was nothing about Jonathan that suggested his sexual inclinations might lie in that direction.

In another century he would have been a philosopher, perhaps.

However much her mother might criticise his

shabby clothes and untidy appearance, Sophy liked him. Perhaps because he made no sexual demands of her, she admitted inwardly. Her conviction as a teenager that she was ugly and plain had long been vanquished when she had gone to university and realised there that men found her attractive; that there was something that challenged them about her almost gypsyish looks. A friend had told her she was 'sexy' but if she was, it was only on the surface, and by the time she had left university she was already accepting that sexually there was something wrong. When a man touched her she felt no spark of desire, nothing but a swift sensation of going back in time to Chris's bed and the despair and misery she had experienced there.

Just before she met Jonathan she had been involved with a man she had met through her father—one of his clients, newly divorced with two small children. She had been drawn to him because he was that little bit older ... but the moment he touched her it had been the old story and that was when she had decided it was pointless trying any longer. Mentally she might be attracted to the male sex but physically she repulsed them.

When she brought her car to a halt on the gravel drive to Jon's house, the children were waiting for her, David grinning happily, Alexandra at his side.

'Uncle Jon's in his study,' David informed her.

'No, he's not' Alex was looking at the house. 'He's coming now.'

All three of them turned to watch the man approaching them. He was wearing the baggy cord jeans her mother so detested and a woollen shirt despite the heat of the day. His hair was ruffled, his expression faintly harassed.

He was one of the few men she had to look up to, Sophy reflected, tilting her head as he approached. She was five-feet-ten, but Jon was well over six foot with unexpectedly broad shoulders. She frowned, registering that fact for the first time, totally thrown when he said unexpectedly, 'Rugger.'

Her mouth fell slightly open. Previously she had thought him one of the dimmest men she had ever met when it came to following other people's thought patterns and that he should so easily have picked up on hers made her stare at him in dazed disbelief. It really was unfair that any man should have such long, dark lashes, she thought idly ... and such beautiful eyes. If Jonathan didn't wear glasses women would fall in love with him by the score for his eyes alone. They were a dense, dark blue somewhere between royal and navy. She had never seen eyes that colour on anyone before.

It wasn't that Jonathan wasn't physically attractive, she mused, suddenly realising that fact. He was! It was just that he carried about him a total air of non-sexuality.

'Louise has gone,' Alexandra told her importantly, tugging on her hand and interrupting her thought train. 'I expect it was because she fell in love with Uncle Jon like the others,' she added innocently.

While Sophy was gaping at her, totally floored by her remark, David remarked sagely, 'No ... it was because Uncle Jon wouldn't let her sleep in his bed. I heard him saying so.'

Conscious of a sudden surge of colour crawling

up over her skin Sophy stared at Jonathan. He looked as embarrassed as she felt, rubbing his jaw, looking away from her as he cleared his throat and said, 'Uh ... I think you two better go inside.'

It couldn't be true. David must have misunderstood, Sophy thought, still trying to take in the mind-boggling implications of the little boy's innocent statement.

She forced herself to look at Jonathan. He was regarding her with apprehension and ... and what ... what exactly did that faint glint at the back of his eyes denote? Sophy mentally pictured Louise. Small, petite with black hair and a pixieish expression, the other girl had exuded sexuality and, from the brief conversations Sophy had exchanged with her, she had gained the impression that the other girl had men coming out of her ears.

Jonathan hadn't denied his nephew's innocent revelation, however. She studied him covertly, suddenly and inexplicably granted another mental image. This time it contained Jonathan as well as Louise ... a Jonathan somewhat unnervingly different from the one she was used to seeing; his body naked and entwined with that of the other girl's.

Sophy blinked and the vision, thankfully, was gone, Jonathan was restored to his normal self. There was that strange glint in his eyes again though but his voice when he spoke was familiarly hesitant and faintly apologetic.

'I believe she had some strange notion about, er ... compelling me to marry her. She wants a rich husband you know.'

Sophy's mind balked a little at taking it all in. That Louise should attempt to seduce Jonathan, of all people, into offering her marriage, seemed impossibly ludicrous. Surely she realised, as Sophy herself had, that he was immune to sexual desire . . . totally oblivious to it in fact.

Another thought struck her. 'And the other two nannies?' she asked faintly.

'Well they didn't actually go to Louise's lengths, but——'

Sophy was too amazed to be tactful. 'But surely they could see that you aren't interested in sex?' she protested.

The dark head bent, and she watched him rub his jaw in his familiar vague fashion, his expression concealed from her as he responded in a faintly strangled voice that betrayed his embarrassment.

'Uh . . . obviously they didn't have your perception.'

'Well next time you'll have to employ someone older,' Sophy told him forthrightly. 'Do you want me to get in touch with the agencies while you're away?'

'Er . . . no. We'll leave it until I get back. Can you stay with them until then?'

'Well yes . . . but why delay?'

'Well I'm thinking about making some other arrangements.'

Other arrangements. What other arrangements? Sophy wondered. As far as she knew, he was the children's only family. Unless—her blood ran cold.

'You're not thinking of abandoning them . . . of putting them into foster homes?'

'Of course . . . of course, it's always a possibility.'

Trying to come to terms with her shock, Sophy

wondered why she had the feeling that he had set
out to say one thing and had ended up saying
another . . . perhaps he was embarrassed to admit
the truth to her. 'Surely there must be another
way,' she said impulsively. 'Something . . .'

'Well there is,' he looked acutely uncomfortable.
'In fact I was going to discuss it with you when I
came back from Brussels.'

'Well why can't you tell me now?'

There were times when his vagueness infuriated
her and now was one of them.

'Well . . . this evening perhaps, when the kids are
in bed.'

It was only natural that he wouldn't want them
to overhear what he might have to say and so she
nodded her head. 'All right then.'

It was nine o'clock before both children were
bathed and in bed. Jonathan's case was packed, his
documents neatly organised and safely bestowed in
his briefcase. He had offered to make them both a
mug of coffee while Sophy finished this final chore
and she had urged him to do so. Up until then he had
been hovering like a demented bloodhound in his
study, frantically searching for some all important
piece of paper which had ultimately turned up under
the telephone. Gritting her teeth, Sophy set about
tidying up. Talk about disorganised!

And yet for all his vagueness, Jon could be
ruthless enough when the occasion demanded it,
she mused, pausing for a moment—witness his
dismissal of Louise.

She sat down in his desk chair, still half stunned
that a girl as clever and as quick as Louise had
honestly thought she could use her sexual allure to
trap Jonathan into marriage. That must have been

what she had thought. No girl as modern as the children's nanny had been could possibly have believed that any man would marry her simply because he had been to bed with her.

Getting up, she made her way to the sitting-room most used by the family. It caught the afternoon sun and she passed by the deeply sashed Victorian windows staring at the sunset as she waited for Jonathan.

'Coffee, Sophy.'

For such a large man he moved extremely quietly. Frowning as she turned round, Sophy was suddenly struck by the fact that Jonathan was altogether deceptive. She always thought of him as clumsy and yet when he was working on his computer he could be surprisingly deft. She had thought him too obtuse and involved in his own private thoughts and his work, and yet he was surprisingly perceptive where the children were concerned and this afternoon, when he had answered her unspoken question. He sat down on the ancient, slightly sagging sofa, the springs groaning slightly as they took his weight. Standing up he often looked thin and faintly stooping but he wasn't thin, she realised in sudden surprise as he took off his glasses and, putting them down on the coffee table, stretched his body tiredly so that she could see the way his muscles moved beneath his shirt, and they *were* muscles, too . . .

Still standing by the window she continued to watch him, faintly shocked to realise that in profile his features were attractively irregular and very masculine. Without his glasses he looked different from the normally aesthetic man he appeared to be. He ceased stretching and rubbed his eyes.

'What have you got planned for the children, Jon?'

She sounded more belligerent than she had intended and she half expected him to jump uneasily in apprehension as he was wont to do when she complained because he had upset her neat filing cabinets. Instead, he smiled at her glintingly.

'You sould like a protective mother hen. Come and sit down. I hate having to look up at you,' he added, smiling again. 'I'm not used to it.'

Knowing that she would not get a scrap more information from him until she did as he asked, Sophy took a chair opposite the settee. Beneath that vague exterior lurked a will of iron, as she already knew, but so far she had only seen it in force where his work was concerned.

Suddenly and quite inexplicably she felt tense and nervous, neither of them feelings she was used to experiencing in Jon's presence. To cover them she said quickly, 'Mother was saying only today that you need a wife, Jon, and I'm beginning to think she's right.'

'So am I.' He started polishing his glasses, something he always did when he was nervous, and yet his nervous movements were oddly at variance with the tense determination she could almost feel emanating from him.

'But not Louise surely?' she began faintly, only to realise that it was hardly any of her business. And yet the thought of the pert, dark-haired young woman as Jon's wife was oddly distasteful to her. She bit her lip and looked up. Jon was looking at her and it was hard to analyse the expression in his eyes. All she did know was that it was unfamiliar to her.

'Not Louise,' he agreed gravely, suddenly looking away from her, his voice once again faintly husky and nervous as he cleared his throat and said, totally out of the blue, 'As a matter of fact, Sophy, I was rather hoping that you . . .'

Her? Jonathan was trying to say that he wanted to marry her! Oh no, surely she must be imagining things. She must have misunderstood. She looked across at him and saw from the hopeful, hesitant look he was giving her that she had not.

'You want to marry me?' she asked disbelievingly, just to be sure. 'You think we should get married? But that's totally out of the question.'

She had expected him to accept her refusal immediately; even to be faintly embarrassed and perhaps a little relieved by it. After all, he could have no real desire to be married to her . . . but to her dismay he shook his head, and plunged on quickly.

'No, no . . . listen to me for a moment. You love the kids.' He paused and while she said nothing Sophy knew she could not deny it. She heard him clearing his throat again and held her breath slightly. 'And, er . . . well . . . that is . . . you don't seem to have a . . . er . . . a boyfriend at the present time.'

'I don't want to get married, Jon,' she broke in firmly. 'Not to you nor to anyone else.'

'But you want children, a family.'

There was no hesitation in his voice this time and once again she was astounded by his perception.

'I need a wife, Sophy,' he continued, 'someone to look after the children and to run my home but not someone to . . . to share my bed.'

The words sank in slowly.

'You mean a ... a marriage of convenience?' Sophy asked him uncertainly. 'Is that legal ... is ...?'

'Perfectly, since no one will know the truth apart from ourselves.'

'But Jonathan, it's crazy! Just because Louise ... is that why you want to marry me?' she asked, staring at him. 'To stop——'

'It's amazing the lengths some of your sex will go to, to secure what they consider to be a wealthy husband and I'm afraid I am wealthy, Sophy.'

She knew that, and while it had never particularly concerned her she could see, now that he had mentioned it, that he would be quite a financial catch for a woman wanting to marry only for money. Suddenly she felt quite protective towards him.

'The children need you as well, Sophy,' he told her. 'They love you. With you they would be secure.'

'If I don't agree, what will you do ... put them in some sort of institution?'

Her mouth went dry at the thought. It was true, she thought bleakly, feeling the pain invade her heart. She did love them ... perhaps all the more so because she knew she would never have any of her own.

She watched Jonathan shrug uncomfortably and get up to pace the room. 'What else can I do?' he asked her. 'You know how much time I spend away. It's not fair to them. They need a settled background. They need you, Sophy. *I* need you.'

'To protect you from the likes of Louise.' Sophy agreed drily, adding teasingly, 'Is the thought of an attractive young woman wanting to seduce you really so very repulsive, Jon?' She knew the moment the words left her lips that they were the wrong ones.

Slow colour crawled up under his skin and he turned away from her saying, in a faintly stifled voice, 'I must confess, I do find such determined young women ... er ... intimidating. I had a very domineering mother,' he added almost apologetically.

Busy drawing the inevitable Freudian conclusions it was several seconds before Sophy observed the faintly risible gleam in his eyes and then it was so brief that she decided she must be imagining it. After all what could Jon be laughing at? It was no laughing matter for a man to have to admit he was frightened of the female sex. After all, didn't she herself hold an almost equal fear of his own, albeit for different reasons. Temptingly the thought slid into her mind that as Jon's wife she would be safe for all time from her own fears about her lack of sexuality. There would be no uncomfortable reminders in her unwed state about her inability to respond to his sex nor any fear that others would discover it and mock her for it as Chris had done.

Chris! No one would ever want to marry her, he had said. She took a deep breath.

'All right then, Jon. I agree. I'll marry you.'

The moment she heard the words she regretted them. Had she gone mad? She couldn't marry Jon. She couldn't but he was already coming towards her, grasping her wrists and hauling her to her feet.

'You will? Sophy, that's marvellous. I can't

thank you enough!' He made no attempt to touch her or to kiss her. Then again, why should he? She wouldn't have wanted him to.

Panic set in. 'Jon . . .'

'I can't tell you what this means to me, to be able to keep the children.'

The children. They would be her family. Already she loved them and found them a constant source of delight. She would have this house, its vast sprawling garden . . . a whole new way of life which she knew instinctively would delight her. She was no ardent career woman and it was a fallacy these days that housewives and mothers degenerated into cabbages. She would have the constant stimulation of the children's growing minds.

But to marry Jon of all people. She glanced at his tall, slightly stooping frame. Wasn't Jon the ideal husband for her, though? an inner voice asked. Jon, whose lack of sexuality would always ensure that he never learned of her humiliating secret. With Jon there would be no fear of rejection or contempt. Jon wouldn't care that sexually she was frigid—wasn't that the word—she goaded herself. Wasn't frigid the description of herself she was always shying away from, fighting against facing, but the truth nonetheless?

'I . . . er, thought we might be married by special licence. Perhaps next weekend?'

Special licence. Sophy came out of her daze to stare at him. 'In such a rush. Is that necessary?'

Jon looked apologetic. 'Well, it would save me having to find a new nanny. You can't stay on here, living here while I'm living here too if we're going to get married, Sophy,' he told her with surprising firmness.

She wanted to laugh. She *was* going to laugh, Sophy thought, on a rising wave of hysteria.

Catching back her nervous giggles she expostulated, 'Jon, this is the nineteen-eighties. You're talking like someone out of the Victorian era.'

'Your mother wouldn't think so.'

His shrewdness left her lost for words for a moment. He was quite right. Her mother would most definitely not approve of her living beneath Jon's roof once she knew they were getting married. Neither, she realised hollowly, would her mother be at all pleased by the fact that they *were* getting married. She closed her eyes, imagining the scenes and recriminations. Jon was not her mother's idea of what she wanted for a son-in-law. She would also want a large wedding with Sophy in traditional white, a June wedding with a marquee and ...

Groaning slightly she opened her eyes and said faintly, 'Yes, you're right. A special licence would be best and then we needn't tell anyone until afterwards.'

There was a strange gleam in Jon's eyes and this time she was almost sure it wasn't the sunset, reflecting off his glasses, that caused it.

'I'll, er ... make all the arrangements then. Do you want to tell the kids or ...?'

'I'll tell them tomorrow when you're gone,' she suggested. 'They're always a bit down after you leave, it will cheer them up a bit.'

Although outwardly well adjusted and cheerful children, Sophy knew that neither of them could have gone through the experience of losing their parents without some scars. They were both

passionately attached to Jon and she had thought
him equally devoted to them. It had shocked her
immensely to hear him talk of sending them away
... it didn't equate with what she knew of his
character somehow.

'I, er ... think I'll have an early night,' she
heard him saying. 'My flight's at nine and I'll have
to be at the airport for eight.'

'Do you want me to drive you?' Jon did not
possess a car; he could neither drive nor, it seemed,
had any desire to do so, although he had hired a
small car for Louise's use.

'No. I've ordered a taxi. Don't bother to get up
to see me off.'

Picking up their coffee cups, Sophy grimaced
slightly to herself. She always saw him off on his
journeys because she lived in perpetual dread that
if she did not he would lose or forget something of
vital importance. She made a mental note to tell
the cab driver to check the taxi before Jon got out
of it and then, bidding him goodnight, carried
their cups to the kitchen.

She was tired herself. It had, after all, been an
eventful day. On her way to the room she always
had when she stayed over at the house and which
was next to the children's room, she had to walk
past Jon's room. As she did so, she hesitated, still
amazed to think that Louise had actually gone
into that room fully intent on making love to its
occupant. That earlier and extraordinarily disturbing mental vision she had had of their bodies
sensuously entwined she had somehow managed to
forget.

CHAPTER TWO

SHE was awake at half-past-seven, showering quickly in the bathroom off her bedroom. The room which she occupied was what the estate agent had euphemistically described as 'a guest suite'. Certainly her bedroom was large enough to house much more than the heavy Victorian furniture it did and it did have its own bathroom but after all that it fell rather short of the luxury conjured up by the description bestowed on it.

She dressed quickly in her jeans and a clean T-shirt. Her body, once gawky and ungainly, had filled out when she reached her twenties and now she had a figure she knew many women might have envied; full breasted, narrow waisted, with long, long legs, outwardly perhaps, as her friend had once teased, 'sexy', but inwardly . . . She was like a cake that was all tempting icing on the outside with nothing but stodge on the inside, she thought wryly, pulling a brush through her hair and grimacing at the crackle of static from it.

There wasn't time to pin it up and she left it curling wildly on to her shoulders, her face completely devoid of make-up and surprisingly young-looking in the hazy sunshine of the summer morning.

As she went past Jon's door she heard the hum of his razor and knew that he was up. Downstairs she checked that the cases she had packed for him the previous night were there in the hall. In the kitchen she ground beans and started making coffee. Jon was not an early morning person, preferring to rise late and work, if necessary, all through the night and despite the fact that she knew he would do no more than gulp down a cup of stingingly hot black coffee, she found and poured orange juice and started to make some toast.

He didn't look surprised to find her in the kitchen, and she knew from his engrossed expression that he was totally absorbed in whatever problem was taking him to Brussels.

Jon was the computer industry's equivalent of the oil world's 'trouble shooter'. She had once heard one of his colleagues saying admiringly that there was nothing Jon did not know about a computer. Although she knew that Jon himself would have been mildly amused by her lack of logic, she herself would have described his skill as something approaching a deep empathy with the machines he worked on.

As far as she was concerned the computer world was a total mystery but she was a good organiser, an excellent secretary and Jon found her flair for languages very useful. He himself seemed to rely entirely on the odd word, nearly always excruciatingly mispronounced from what Sophy could discover. But then, who needed words to communicate with a computer? Logic was what was needed there ... and Jon had plenty of that, she thought wryly as she poured and passed his coffee. Only a man of supreme logic would propose to a woman on the strength of needing her to look after his wards and run his home. And also to keep other women out of his bed, Sophy reminded herself.

She didn't ask him if he wanted toast, simply pushing the buttered golden triangles in front of him. He picked one up, absently bit into it and then, frowning, put it down.

'You know I don't eat breakfast.'

'Then you should,' she reproved him. 'It's no wonder you're so thin.' But he wasn't, she remembered . . . recollecting that brief, unexpected glimpse of hard muscles.

She heard the sound of a car approaching over the gravel. So did Jon. He stood up, swallowing the last of his coffee.

'I'll ring you on Wednesday to let you know what time I get back. If anything urgent crops up in the meantime——'

'I know where to get in touch with you,' she assured him. She would have to drive into Cambridge later and leave a message on the office answering service asking callers to ring her here at the house. Her mind raced ahead, busily engaged in sorting out the host of minor problems her being here instead of in Cambridge would cause.

She walked with Jon to the taxi . . . sighing in faint exasperation as he forgot to pick up his briefcase, handing it to him through the open door and then turning to speak to the driver.

'Ticket . . .' she intoned automatically, turning back to Jon. 'Passport, money . . .'

He patted the pocket of his ancient tweed jacket, a faintly harassed look crossing his face.

Registering and interpreting it correctly Sophy instructed. 'Stay there, I'll go and get them.'

She found them in a folder beside his bed, and sighed wryly. She remembered quite distinctly handing them to him yesterday and telling him to put them in his jacket pocket.

She ran downstairs and handed the documents to him, catching the driver's eye as she did so. He was looking faintly impatient.

'I'll see you late Wednesday or early Thursday.' She closed the taxi door and waited until it had turned out of the drive.

Back in the kitchen she munched absently at Jon's toast and drank her coffee. She and Jon were to be married. It was incredible, ridiculous ... only strangely it didn't seem that way. Already she felt an oddly comfortable pleasure in the thought, as though some burden of pressure had been released. She *wanted* to marry him, she realised with a start of surprise ... or at least ... she wanted what marriage to him would give her. She frowned. Didn't that mean that in her way she was just as selfishly grasping as Louise? But, unlike Louise, she did care about Jon. As a person she liked him very much indeed. As a man he was so totally unthreatening to her that she found his company relaxing. Marriage to Jon would be like slipping into a pair of comfortable slippers ... But on Saturday? She comforted herself with the thought that it was hardly likely that Jon would be able to organise a special licence so quickly. In fact she doubted he would even remember about it once he got on the plane. No doubt the task of sorting out all the arrangements would fall to her once he came back but she would still prefer not to tell her parents until after the ceremony.

Coward, she mocked herself, hearing sounds from upstairs that meant David and Alex were up and about.

She told them about Jon's proposal after breakfast. All three of them were outside, sitting on the lawn. Their open delight and excitement made tears sting her eyes. David flung his arms round her embracing her exuberantly, Alex hanging on to her arm.

'I'm glad he's marrying you and not that nasty old Louise,' she told Sophy. 'We didn't like her, did we, David?'

'No, and neither did Uncle Jon . . . otherwise he would have let her sleep in his bed.' A thought seemed to strike him. 'Does that mean you'll be sleeping in his bed, Sophy?'

A strange paralysis seemed to have gripped her. She wasn't sure how much the children knew about adult behaviour. They must have learned something from school but their parents had been dead for three years and she could hardly see Jon satisfactorily explaining the so-called facts of life to them. On the other hand, it was pointless telling them a lie.

'No, I won't, David,' she said at last.

She watched him frown and saw that for some reason her answer had not pleased him.

'That's because both of you are so big, I expect,' intervened Alex, ever practical. 'You wouldn't both get in one bed.'

'They would in Uncle Jon's,' David told her gruffly. 'It's huge.'

It was . . . king size and Jon normally slept diagonally across it. She knew because she occasionally had to wake him up in the morning when he had an early business appointment and he had been up late the previous night working. She had never needed to do much more than lightly touch his duvet mummy-wrapped body though.

'If you're going to get married, why won't you be sleeping in his bed?' he persisted doggedly.

'Married people don't always share the same bed, David,' she told him, giving him what she hoped was a reassuring smile. 'You know what your uncle's like. He often works very late and I like to go to bed early. He would wake me up and then I wouldn't be able to get back to sleep.'

He looked far from convinced, muttering, 'Ladies always sleep with their husbands,' and betraying a innate chauvinism that made Sophy smile. Already at ten he was very, very sure in his masculinity and of its supremacy which was surely something he didn't get from Jon. He was also, as she had often observed, very protective of his sister . . . and too, of her. She bent forward and ruffled his dark hair.

'Perhaps Uncle Jon doesn't want her to sleep with him, David,' Alex offered, smiling at him. 'He didn't want Louise to.'

The little girl was more right than she knew, Sophy thought grimly, glad of the distraction of the telephone ringing.

As she had half suspected it was her mother, eager to tell her all about the previous evening's dinner party.

'Chris came too,' she told Sophy, oblivious to her daughter's lack of enthusiasm, 'and he brought his wife. Such a lovely girl . . . tiny with masses of blonde curls and so obviously in love with him. She's expecting their first baby. He asked after you, and didn't seem at all surprised to hear you weren't married.' There was a hint of reproof in her mother's voice. 'He even laughed about it.'

Sophy realised as she replaced the receiver that she was actually grinding her teeth. So he had laughed, had he? Well, he would soon stop laughing when he heard that she *was* married! She stood motionless by the telephone staring blindly out of the study window for a few seconds picturing the ordeal the dinner party would have been for her had she been there ... that future dinner parties would have been if it hadn't been for Jon's extraordinary proposal. Without being aware of it he had saved her from the most galling humiliation and pain. Now she needn't even see Chris, never mind endure his mocking taunts on her unmarried state.

Over the next couple of days, cautiously at first and then with growing confidence, like someone blessedly discovering the cessation of toothache and then cautiously exploring the previously tormented area and finding it blissfully whole again, Sophy allowed herself to acknowledge the totally unexpected happiness unfurling inside her.

The children were a constant, sometimes funny, sometimes exasperating joy and one she had never thought to know. For some women the physical act of giving birth was acutely necessary to motherhood but she, it seemed, was not one of them. She could not take the place of the children's dead mother and did not seek to but it gave her a special delight to know that she would have the joy of mothering them. It was this, probably more than anything else, that convinced her that her decision to marry Jon was the right one. She still didn't know how he could even have thought of relinquishing his responsibility for them but then his mind was so wrapped up in his work, that everything else was obviously secondary to it.

On Tuesday evening it rained and they spent the evening going through some old photograph albums David had found in a bureau drawer.

Once she and Jon were married she would ask him if she was to be allowed a free hand with the house, Sophy mused, glancing round the shabby sitting room, and mentally transforming it with new furnishings. At the present moment in time it wasn't even particularly comfortable. Both the sofa and the chairs had loose springs which dug into vulnerable flesh if sat upon.

'Look Sophy, there's Daddy and Uncle Jon when they were little.'

Sophy glanced down at the open page of the album, her eyes widening fractionally as she studied the photograph Alex was pointing out.

Two lanky adolescent boys stood side by side, one topping the other by a couple of inches. Both of them had identical shocks of near black hair—both of them had the same regular features, hinting at formidably good looks in adulthood.

'Uncle Jon looks really like Daddy there, doesn't he?' Alex commented, wrinkling her nose. 'He doesn't look anything like Daddy did now though, does he, David?'

Thus applied to, her brother studied the photograph briefly and then said gruffly. 'Yes he does ... underneath.'

It was an odd remark for the little boy to make and one, Sophy sensed, made in defence of his uncle against his sister's comment.

'Uncle Jon would look much better without his

glasses,' Alex continued cheerfully. 'He should wear contact lenses like our teacher at school.'

'He can't,' David told her loftily. 'They don't suit his eyes, and besides, he doesn't need to wear his glasses all the time anyway.'

This was news to Sophy. She had never seen him without them, apart from one occasion she recalled, remembering watching him remove them here in this very room. Then she had been struck by the very male attractiveness of his profile, she remembered and then shrugged mentally. What did it matter what Jon looked like? It was the kind of man he *was* that was important. She already knew all about the pitfalls encountered in getting involved with handsome men. Chris was good looking.

On the Wednesday morning after she had dropped the children off at school she got back just in time to hear the 'phone ringing noisily.

Thinking it might be Jon, she rushed inside and picked up the receiver, speaking slightly breathlessly into it, barely registering her sudden spearing disappointment at discovering it wasn't him as she listened to the crisp American tones of the man on the other end of the line.

She explained to him that Jon was due back that day, and slowly read back to him the message he had given her, frowning slightly as she did so.

She knew, of course, that Jon often did work for various governments, but that call had been from the Space Center in Nassau, where apparently they were urgently in need of Jon's expertise.

Would that mean he had to fly straight out to Nassau, before they could get married? She shrugged slightly. It didn't really matter when the ceremony took place, surely?

The next time the 'phone rang it was Jon, ringing her from the airport in Brussels, to tell her the time of his flight.

'I managed to get through a little earlier than planned,' he told her, adding, 'any messages?'

Quickly Sophy told him about the call from Nassau, giving him the number and asking hesitantly, 'Will that mean that you'll have to fly straight out there?'

There was a pause so long that she thought at one point their connection had been cut and then Jon said slowly, 'I'm not sure.' Having re-checked with him the number of his flight, Sophy said goodbye and replaced the receiver.

She would have to ring Heathrow now and check what time it was due to arrive . . . her mind ran on, mentally ticking off all that would have to be done. The children would have to be collected from school, fed . . . Yet all the time at the back of her mind was that same ridiculous sense of apprehension.

Suppose Jon had changed his mind about wanting to marry her? How long would he need to be in Nassau? What if he . . .?

Stop it! she urged herself firmly, reminding herself that less than a week ago there had been no thought in her mind of marriage to anyone, let alone her boss and now here she was in a mild flurry of panic in case they did not marry.

Since the time needed to get to Heathrow and back to meet Jon's flight interfered with the children's school leaving time, and because she knew of no one she could ask to meet them in her place, Sophy rang the school and asked to speak with the headmistress, quickly explaining the

situation and getting permission to collect David
and Alex on her way to Heathrow just after lunch.

Neither of them stopped chattering during the
drive. Oddly enough, this would be the first time
either of them had been to the airport and since
Sophy always believed in having a little time in
hand once they had parked the car she was able to
take them to the viewing gallery to watch the
flights taking off and landing.

'Will we see Uncle Jon's plane from up here?'
David demanded at one point.

Sophy glanced at her watch. Jon's flight was due
in in five minutes.

'Yes,' she told him. 'We'll watch it land and
then we'll go down to the arrivals lounge to wait
for him.

The flight was on time and the plane landed
perfectly, so there was no reason for her to feel
that odd choking sensation of fear clutch at her
throat, Sophy chided herself, especially when she
had already watched half a dozen or so planes
come and go without the slightest trace of
apprehension.

'Look! Look, Sophy ... they're putting the
stairs up,' Alex told her excitedly, tugging on
her hand. 'Can we wait and see Uncle Jon get
off?'

Sophy knew from past experience that Jon was
likely to be the last to leave the plane but in the
face of the little girl's excitement she could hardly
refuse. It would be a bit of a rush down to the
arrivals lounge ... and she always liked to be on
hand just in case Jon ran into any problems. There
had been that time he had left his passport on the
plane and another when he had lost the keys for

his briefcase, and the strange buzzing sound emanating from it had drawn frowns and stern looks from the security authorities. In the end it had simply been the alarm he had forgotten to switch off but . . .

'All right,' she agreed, 'but then we'll have to rush back down.'

'Look . . . they're getting off now,' David called out, 'but I can't see Uncle Jon.'

As Sophy had guessed, Jon was the last off the plane, a clutch of dark suited business men in front of him, the whole party impeded by the slow progress of an old lady who was having difficulty walking.

One of them, obviously growing impatient, pushed past her. His companions followed suit, and Sophy felt an impotent cry of warning rise in her throat as she saw the old lady lose her balance.

What happened next was so out of character that for a moment or two she actually doubted the evidence of her own eyes.

Jon who never seemed to be aware of what was going on around him . . . Jon who could often be so clumsy and awkward, moved forward so quickly that Sophy blinked. He caught the old lady before she could fall, supporting her with one arm while he held on to his briefcase with the other. She had never seen anyone move so quickly, Sophy reflected, nor move with such controlled reflexes, unless it was on the sports field.

'Gosh, did you see the way Uncle Jon saved that lady?' Alex asked, round-eyed. 'It was really fast, wasn't it?'

'That's because of playing rugger,' David

informed her loftily. 'He used to play when he was at Cambridge.'

'And he did rowing as well,' Alex chipped in, as Sophy drew them away from the viewing windows and towards the arrivals lounge.

She had known about the rugby but it had never occurred to her to think of Jon as an athletic man. Chris who prided himself on his physical fitness spent at least three evenings per week in the gym, jogged and played amateur football but, as far as she knew, Jon did none of these things. There were of course those totally unexpected muscles shaping his shoulders and chest though. Irritated with herself without knowing why, Sophy tried to re-direct her thoughts.

For once, Jon managed to negotiate the hazards of passport control and baggage checks without any mishaps.

As he came through the gate Alex slipped her hand from Sophy's and ran towards him. Watching him field her as easily as any rugby ball and transfer his baggage to his other hand, Sophy was forced to admit that there were obviously still some aspects of her future husband that she was not familiar with. The knowledge was a little unsettling. Up until now she had thought she knew Jon very well indeed and had been quite content with the slightly exasperated toleration which was the normal feeling he aroused within her. Indeed she liked feeling faintly motherly and superior to him, she realised. Thoroughly startled by this sudden discovery about herself, she was the last of the trio to step forward and greet him.

'That was really good how you saved that old lady from falling, Uncle Jon,' David was saying.

'We watched you from the gallery, didn't we, Sophy?'

Over David's head the navy blue eyes fixed rather myopically and vaguely on her own.

Alex piped up, 'Yes, Sophy was so surprised that her mouth was open—like this.' She demonstrated Sophy's stunned surprise far too well, the latter thought uncomfortably, feeling the slow crawl of embarrassed colour seeping up under her skin as Jon continued to look at her.

Her embarrassment heightened when David asked suddenly, 'Aren't you going to kiss Sophy, Uncle Jon? You can do now that you're going to get married.'

'I don't think I will right now, old son, if you don't mind.' Watching Jon ruffle David's hair and listening to the mild, even tone of his voice as he side-tracked his nephew away from such a potentially embarrassing subject, Sophy knew she should be grateful to Jon for what he had done but for some strange reason, what she was really feeling, if she was honest, was a sense of genuine pique. Jon couldn't have made it more plain that the thought of kissing her held absolutely no appeal for him, she thought irrationally. Was she really so unattractive to him that . . .? She stopped abruptly, stunned by the train of her own thoughts. Of course Jon did not want to kiss her— her or anyone else . . . indeed that was the reason she had felt able to agree to marry him. So why . . .?

It must be something to do with all the re-united couples and families freely embracing around them that had aroused that momentary and totally unnecessary fit of pique inside her. Feeling much better now that she had found a logical explanation for her irrational feelings, Sophy hurried to catch up with the others and led the way to where she had parked the car.

CHAPTER THREE

IT was gone ten o'clock, the silence in the study as they both worked a companionable one and then Jon got up and walked over to the window, his back to her as he stared out into the garden. His hair had grown slightly while he was away, Sophy noticed absently and it looked better, even curling faintly into his nape.

'Will you have to fly out to Nassau immediately?' she asked him suddenly, uneasy with the silence she had found so relaxing only seconds before.

He turned round and smiled mildly. 'No, not straight away. Not until Sunday.'

'So . . .' All at once her throat was dry. 'So you'll still be here for the wedding, then?' Fool, idiot, she derided herself mentally; without him there wouldn't *be* a wedding and she had made him sound like one of the guests.

'Oh, yes . . . I've made all the arrangements. Got the special licence organised through someone I know in Brussels.'

'You're not having second thoughts, then?'

Good heavens, what was the matter with her? What was she asking him for? She was behaving like a total fool.

'No. Are you?'

It was unusual for Jon to ask such a direct question and in such a crisp tone. She shook her head without looking at him, suddenly too restless to stay in her seat. She got up and paced a few steps.

'There is one thing though.' She tensed. 'When we were discussing the ... er ... style of our marriage I neglected to mention one point.'

'Yes?' Her mouth felt frozen and stiff, so much so that it was difficult to shape the word.

'We have discussed my reasons for our marriage, Sophy but I don't think we've fully discussed yours. I know you care deeply for the children,' he went on before she could speak, 'but—and please correct me if I am wrong—you could always have children of your own. No, please,' he stopped her when she would have spoken. 'You are, in addition, a very attractive woman.' He saw her expression and his mouth twisted slightly. 'I assure you, Sophy, that even my shortsightedness is not sufficient to blind me to that fact. A woman whom I am sure very many members of my sex would be only too pleased to marry. Men who would want to share with you a far more intimate relationship than the one I am offering.'

It was ridiculous to feel embarrassed but she was.

'I don't want that kind of relationship,' she managed to say thickly, turning away from him.

'I see. This is, I presume, because of the romantic involvement you once had with someone else. You did tell me some such thing the first time we met,' he reminded her.

Her face flamed. She had had so much to drink that night she could not remember what she had told him, but it embarrassed her now to think that she had probably poured out to him all her maudlin misery over what had once been her love for Chris.

'I take it there is no question of this, er ... relationship——'

'None at all,' Sophy managed to interrupt huskily.

'I see. Having suffered the pangs of love once and been hurt by it you have no wish to risk yourself with such an emotion again, is that it?'

It wasn't because she was frightened of *loving* that she was marrying him, Sophy reflected, but it was much simpler and easier to let him believe that than to tell him the truth.

She lifted her head and looked at him, forcing a cool smile. 'Yes, Jon, that is it. The relationship you are offering me, the chance to take over the role of mother to the children, is exactly what I want.'

'Very well ... but I must tell you, Sophy, that, er ... that there can be no question of me tolerating a sexual relationship which you might form outside our marriage.'

'You mean you wouldn't want me to take a lover?'

'Yes, that is exactly what I mean.'

It was getting dark and in the dusk she could barely see across the room.

The aura that Jon projected when she was not able to see him clearly was unnervingly at odds with the man she knew him to be. Even his voice seemed to have changed, become slightly silky and somehow subtly menacing.

'You have my word that there will be no question of that, Jon,' she told him quietly and truthfully. Not wanting him to ask any more questions she gave a small shrug and added lightly, 'Perhaps, like yourself, I am one of those humans whose sex drive is so low as to be almost non-existent.'

She thought for a moment he seemed to tense, as though about to say something and wondered uncertainly if she had perhaps hurt or offended him by being so frank. No man would enjoy hearing himself described as virtually sexless, she thought guiltily.

'And this man . . . the one you loved, Sophy?'

'He's married now. It would never have worked. He didn't . . .' she swallowed and told what was in effect merely a half lie. 'He didn't care in the way that I did.'

Suddenly and inexplicably she felt quite exhausted. 'It's been a long day, Jon,' she told him quietly. 'If you don't mind, I think I'll go to bed.'

She knew it would be a long time before Jon came upstairs and, although he smiled vaguely at her as she went out of the room, she sensed that his mind was already on other things.

It had never occurred to her that he might question her motives in agreeing to marry him and was relieved that he had assumed that it was her non-existent love for Chris that had motivated her. It rather surprised her that he should remember her wine-induced confidences on the night of the party when they first met. She had been feeling particularly down at the time otherwise she would never have said a word.

'So are you really and truly married now?'

Sophy nodded her head, and smiled at Alex. She

was still quite amazed that Jon had managed to
arrange the details without any hitch.

She had also been a little surprised at his
insistence on a religious ceremony but had said
nothing. In all honesty she had to admit there had
been something comforting and right about the
familiar Church service that had soothed away a
lot of her last minute doubts. Now it was too late.
They were married, Jon looking exceedingly
uncomfortable in a suit he must surely have had
since he came down from university and so heavy
that it was totally unsuitable for a hot July day, she
thought exasperatedly.

'I'm going to have to do something about your
clothes,' she told him wryly. 'They're atrocious.'

'Are they?' He stared vaguely at her, frowningly
perplexed, and yet as he turned his head slightly to
answer a question David had asked him, Sophy
was sure she saw his mouth curl faintly in
amusement. What had she said to amuse him?
Nothing, surely?

There was no question of a honeymoon of
course. Jon was flying to Nassau in the morning
and following the early morning wedding ceremony
Sophy intended to spend the afternoon checking
that everything was in order for his trip. 'I'll have
to give my mother a ring and tell her the news,' she
murmured, blenching a little at the thought of that
ordeal.

'Er, no. I think it would be better if we drove
over there now and I told her.'

She stared at Jon unable to believe her ears. Jon
was terrified of her mother.

'Jon, there's really no need,' she began.

'I think there's every need.' The cool firmness in

his voice silenced her protests and even David and
Alex stopped what they were doing to look at him.
Probably because they were so unused to hearing
their uncle speak in such decisive tones.

'But you don't have time. Your flight——'

'Is all perfectly organised, thanks to my wife.
And we have plenty of time. We'll have a quick
snack lunch and leave straight away. All of us.'

And so it was that at three o'clock in the
afternoon Sophy found herself drawing up outside
her parents' front door. Once she had stopped the
car Jon clambered out, knocking his head as he
did so. The front passenger seat of her car was far
too small for him. It was easy to overlook how big
a man he really was, Sophy reflected, watching
him help the children out.

'You're going to need a larger car.'

'Only when you're travelling in it,' Sophy told
him wryly, leading the way through the garden to
the back of her house, knowing that on such a
lovely day her parents would be in the garden.

They were, but they weren't alone and Sophy
came to an abrupt halt as the ring of her high-
heeled sandals on the crazy paving path caused the
tall blonde man lazing in a deckchair to turn his
head and look at her.

'Sophy . . . good heavens.'

He hadn't changed, Sophy thought, registering
the lazy insolence in his voice, the mockery with
which his glance slid over her body, as though
reminding her that he knew how lacking in
femininity it really was.

'Sophy?' Her mother suddenly appeared through
the french windows, carrying a tray of tea things,
her mouth rounding in astonishment. 'You didn't

say you were coming over this afternoon.' There was just a touch of reproof in her mother's light voice, and Sophy suppressed a faint sigh. Her mother liked everything done by the book, arrangements properly made . . . She should have thought about that.

'It's my fault, I'm afraid, Mrs Marley.'

For the first time since seeing Chris she became conscious of Jon standing beside her.

'Your . . . Oh!' There was no mistaking the displeasure in her mother's voice and Sophy felt her guilt turn into quiet despair.

'Where's Father?' she asked, scanning the garden.

'He's showing Felicity, my wife, the new rose arbour he's building,' Chris answered easily. 'I rather think I shall have to watch my wife, Mrs Marley,' he added charmingly to Sophy's mother, 'I do believe she's falling rather hard for your husband.'

Listening to her mother's girlish trill of laughter, Sophy was overwhelmed by a familiar feeling of alienation. She didn't fit in here in this neat over-tidy garden . . . in this peaceful English family scene. Chris was more at home here than she was, she thought bitterly, and her mother more pleased by his company than she ever was by hers.

'Nonsense, you foolish boy,' she chided Chris. 'Anyone can see that Felicity only has eyes for you. She's so much in love with you.'

She could almost see Chris preening himself under her mother's flattery and suddenly Sophy felt the most acute dislike for him. She had fallen out of love with him a long time ago but this dislike was a new and gloriously freeing thing, giving her the courage to say calmly, 'Mother, there's something I——'

'I think I should be the one to break our news to your parents, Sophy.'

The deep and commanding tones of Jon's voice broke through her own, silencing her. She blinked and turned round to study him, wondering at this sudden assumption of masculine authority, half expecting to see someone else standing behind her. But no, it was still Jon, looking thoroughly hot and uncomfortable in his baggy cords and thick woollen shirt, his glasses catching the sunlight and obscuring his eyes from her.

Their voices had obviously carried down the garden, and Sophy watched her father walking towards them accompanied by Chris's wife. She was every bit as pretty as her mother had said but Sophy felt no envy for her, only a certain wry sympathy. Unless he had changed dramatically, Chris did not have it in him to be loyal and loving to one woman, even one as lovely as this. Her pregnancy barely showed, her light summer dress showing off her summer tan.

'Darling, let me introduce you to an old friend of mine.' Irritatingly it was Chris who took charge of the proceedings, drawing his wife towards him.

'Oh, not another old flame, darling . . . .' The fluttery voice was unexpectedly hard, and instantly Sophy revised her opinion. Chris's wife was not the delicate little flower she looked. On the contrary, she was every bit as hard as Chris himself, she thought inwardly, taking the hand the other girl extended.

'Heavens, aren't you tall!' Innocent blue eyes slid upwards over Sophy's body. 'You must be almost six foot.'

'Five-ten actually.' From somewhere Sophy managed to summon a cool smile. Six foot made her sound like a giantess—a freak almost.

'And this,' Chris was looking past Sophy now to Jon and the children. His mouth curled in a dazzling smile, laughter lighting his eyes as he looked at Jon. 'You can only be Sophy's boss!' His glance swept derisively over Jon's appearance, and Sophy could almost see him comparing it with his own. The immaculate white cotton jeans, the cotton knit jumper in blues and greens banded with white ... the elegantly cool casualness of his appearance in comparison to Jon's.

Chris's rudeness did not surprise her, but the blindingly fierce stab of mingled anger and protectiveness she felt, did. She reached out instinctively to take Jon's hand in her own, unaware of the deeply gold glitter in her eyes as she said firmly, 'And my husband. That's what we came to tell you ... Jon and I were married this morning.'

'Married!' Her mother looked shocked and disbelieving, and Sophy was furious with her when she cried out, 'Oh, Sophy ... no ... how could you do this to us?' her eyes dropping immediately to her daughter's tautly flat stomach.

Fury kicked sharply beneath her heart as Sophy realised what her mother was thinking.

'Sophy is not pregnant, Mrs Marley.' She was still holding Jon's hand and the firmness with which he squeezed her fingers was intensely reassuring. She was beginning to feel as though she had strayed into a bad dream. She had known her parents would not be pleased ... but that her mother should actually think she was pregnant.

She was burning with embarrassment on her parents' behalf. Neither of them had made the slightest attempt to put Jon at ease or to make him feel welcome.

'Then why such a rush?' her mother complained. 'Why didn't you say anything the last time you were here?' She looked suspiciously from her daughter's flushed face to the one of the man behind her. 'I know what it is,' she said shrilly. 'You've married her so that you'll have someone to look after those children. I told you he was making use of you.'

Sophy couldn't endure it. She turned blindly towards Jon saying huskily, 'I think we'd better leave,' but the hard pressure of his hand holding hers held her back.

'You do your daughter a severe injustice, Mrs Marley,' he said very gently. 'I married Sophy quite simply because I love her.'

Even her mother fell silent at that, rallying enough to add huffily, 'Well, I still think you should have told us, Sophy. I can't understand why you should have got married in such a hole-and-corner fashion at all . . . and in such a rush!'

'Because I want to be with Jon and the children, Mother,' she managed evenly. 'That was why.'

'Well you can't expect your father and me not to be shocked. Not even to tell us about the wedding——'

'I had the most wonderful wedding,' Felicity cut in cattily. 'Five hundred guests and a marquee on the lawn at home. Mummy said it was her dream come true for me.'

'Good old Sophy! Married, eh?' Chris was eyeing her with open mockery. 'I never thought I'd

see the day. You know, old boy, I once actually
bet Sophy that she'd never find a man to marry her.'

'Well, you see, you were wrong.'

Was she imagining the faint rasp beneath Jon's
mild tone? She must be, Sophy thought, her skin
suddenly burning with furious anger as she heard
Chris saying quite distinctly to his wife, 'Not as
wrong as all that.' He turned to Jon and taunted
smilingly, 'She told you about our little bet, then,
did she?'

'She may have mentioned it.' Jon looked totally
vague and disinterested. 'But it was a very long
time ago, wasn't it?' He said it so mildly that there
seemed to be no outward reason why Chris should
colour so hotly until Jon added equally mildly,
'Really I'm surprised you even remember it. Sophy
can't have been more than nineteen or so at the
time.'

The children were pressing quietly against her
side, and Sophy turned to her mother pinning a
smile on her face.

'I think we'd better leave now, Mother. Jon has
to fly to Nassau in the morning.'

'*Jon* has to . . .' Chris's eyebrows rose. 'Dear me,
how very unromantic but then no doubt as you're
both living in the same house you've already had
ample opportunity to——'

'Become lovers?' Jon seemed totally oblivious to
Chris's malice. 'Oh, about the same opportunity as
any other couple of our age and situation in life,'
he agreed cheerfully.

'Mummy would never have agreed with me
living with Chris before we were married,' Felicity
chipped in dulcetly, earning an approving glance
from *her* mother, Sophy noted.

'No?' Really, it was quite incredible how Jon's face changed when he removed his glasses. He had been in the act of polishing them when Felicity spoke and there was quite definitely something almost satanic about the way his eyebrow rose and his mouth curled as he looked across at the other girl.

'And we were engaged for twelve months.'

'A wildly passionate romance.'

Sophy couldn't believe her ears. Chris was red to the tips of his ears and an unbecoming tightness had formed round Felicity's bowlike mouth. Sophy was quite sure that Felicity and Chris had been lovers well before the date of their marriage; how could it be otherwise when Chris was such a highly sexed man. She had no doubt that the little act Felicity was putting on was purely for her parents' benefit.

'I think we'd better leave.'

Neither of her parents made any attempt to stop them going but Sophy didn't realise that Jon had misinterpreted the reason for her tiny sigh of relief, as they got in the car and he said in an unusually clipped tone. 'Don't let it bother you, Sophy. The loss is theirs, not yours. Good heavens,' he muttered in a much more Jon-like tone, 'can't they see that you're worth a dozen of that stupid, vain little butterfly?'

Wryly she smiled across at him, and said huskily. 'Thanks ... for everything.' She was remembering how he had claimed that he loved her, protecting her from Chris's malice.

All four of them were subdued on the way back, although it wasn't until the children were in bed and they were alone that Jon again raised the subject of her parents.

'I hope you weren't too hurt by what happened today, Sophy,' he began uncertainly. 'If I had known . . .'

'I stopped being hurt by the fact that I'm not the daughter my parents wanted, a long time ago,' she said calmly. 'But I was angry, Jon . . . angry and embarrassed that they should show such a lack of welcome and politeness to you.'

He shrugged and looked slightly uncomfortable as though the emotion in her voice embarrassed him.

'I don't suppose we'll see that much of them,' he rumbled clearing his throat. 'Er . . . Benson, I suppose he's the one.'

'Yes,' Sophy agreed tightly. 'Yes, he's the one . . . but it's all over now, Jon. My life and loyalty lie with you and the children now.'

'Yes . . .'

Why should she feel that there was a certain wry irony in the way he was looking at her?

Sophy spent the fortnight Jon was away in Nassau organising her new life. From now on Jon would work mainly from home when he was in England, so she moved some of the files from the office in town to his study. She managed to do some fence building in her relationship with her parents but admitted to herself that it could never be the warm one she had once wanted. As she had firmly told her mother, Jon was now her husband and he and the children came first. Grudgingly this had been accepted, but Sophy doubted that there would be much contact between them in future.

She also spent time planning how she was going to refurbish the house. Jon had given her permission to do exactly what she wanted and had also told her she need not stint on cost. She had been a little surprised to discover that he had also organised a new bank account for her and had placed into it what seemed to be an impossibly large sum of money.

She had always known that he was a reasonably wealthy man but she had not realised, until now, exactly how wealthy. Perhaps because Jon himself never looked like an even remotely prosperous man, never mind a rich one.

That was something else she would have to do something about, she decided on the Wednesday before he was due back. She would go through his wardrobe, discover what size he was and start re-stocking it. She still burned with resentment when she thought about the way Chris had looked at him.

If ever she had worried about falling for Chris again she did so no longer. Indeed it amazed her that she could ever have found him the slightest bit attractive. The wounds he had inflicted still hurt but she found the man himself contemptible.

Sophy was familiar enough with the clothes Jon wore not to be too surprised by the collection of hairy suits and worn tweed jackets she discovered in his wardrobe. Rather wryly she wondered what on earth it was about the colour of mud that attracted him so much but other than that, her search was briskly impersonal and she stopped only to check on sizes before closing the wardrobe door and leaving the bedroom. Its furniture, like that in the rest of the house, was of no particular style or beauty. Jon had told her that he had bought it with the house. She planned to get rid of the majority of it, but not until she had decided what was to take its place.

Her decision made, she didn't waste any time. After picking the children up from school she drove briskly towards Cambridge.

'You're going the wrong way,' Alex told her.

Sophy shook her head. 'No I'm not. I want to do some shopping. Your uncle needs some new clothes.'

The silence from the pair in the back seat confirmed Sophy's view that she was far from the only one to note the lack of appeal about Jon's attire.

He must be boiled alive in those heavy cords he favoured and those woollen shirts, especially during the heatwave they were having at the moment.

She wondered wryly how on earth he was getting on in Nassau. When she had remarked that he was going to be hot he had told her that the temperature in computer operational rooms was always maintained at a set point, no matter what the climate.

It didn't take long to park the car and Sophy knew Cambridge well enough to head straight for a small street which housed half a dozen or so exclusive shops catering for both men and women.

She stopped outside the window of one of them surveying the grey blouson jacket with its royal blue lining and the matching, pleated trousers, also trimmed in blue.

'I don't think Uncle Jon would like that,' David informed her doubtfully.

Sophy grinned. She could just picture Jon's face if she produced something as radically modern as that. No, what she had in mind was something rather more conservative.

'Then we won't go in,' she told David equably, herding the pair instead to a shop two doors down which stocked a range of Jaeger clothes for men.

It took her over an hour to make her final choice, which included two shirts, one in silk and one in cotton in a shade of blue which Alex had informed her was exactly the same as Jon's eyes.

Having chosen those it had proved fairly easy to pick out the basis of a new wardrobe for him based almost entirely on blue and cream— including a softly blue herringbone tweed jacket which she was pleased to see bore no resemblance whatsoever to the ones already in his wardrobe.

Having paid the bill and escorted the children outside she remembered that both of them seemed short of casual T-shirts and that she could do with some inexpensive casual wear herself. The heat-wave which had begun in the early part of the month was still persisting with no let-up forecast and her wardrobe was not really geared to such hot weather.

It only took them a few minutes to walk to Marks & Spencer, where she gave in to Alex's entirely feminine whim to be kitted out in a range of separates in pretty pinks. Even David allowed himself to be persuaded into a pair of brushed denim jeans in a soft olive colour to which Sophy added several T-shirts and thin cotton jumpers.

'Look over there. Uncle Jon would like nice in that, Sophy,' Alex informed her, having by now thoroughly entered into the spirit of things.

On the display she had indicated, Sophy could see a range of men's casual separates in a soft, pale sand colour.

She went over to inspect them, trying in her mind's eye to imagine Jon dressed in the well-cut brushed denim jeans and matching bush shirt, the toning grey and sand jumper draped casually over the model's shoulders adorning Jon's, and failed miserably. Even so ... he *was* short of jeans, and she could always bring them back. Recklessly she bought a full outfit, adding socks and the shoes that the assistant pointed out to her, only remembering on the way out that she hadn't got anything for herself.

A rack of pale green cotton shorts with matching patterned short sleeved shirts and plain T-shirts caught her eye, and while she was studying them Alex tugged away from her hand, coming back several seconds later proudly clutching a mint and white bikini plus a pair of matching shorts.

'Look at these, Sophy,' she demanded. 'They would look great with those shorts and things. You could sunbathe in the garden in them.'

It was years since she had worn a bikini—four at least. That was how long it had been since she had last been abroad. She no longer felt so ashamed of her body that she could not bring herself to reveal more of it than actually necessary, but even so ... a bikini?

'I don't ...' she began and then seeing how Alex's face fell, amended her remark quickly, 'I don't see why not! Come on, let's go and pay for all these things, and then as a special treat ...'

'Fish and chips?' they both begged together.

Laughing, she gave way.

'Uncle Jon hardly ever lets us have chips,' David complained on the way home. 'He says they aren't good for you.'

'He's quite right,' Sophy agreed, firmly squashing any hopes David might have that she would not. There was a rather neglected vegetable plot in the garden and she had already tentatively wondered about planting it next year. There was obviously some of her father in her after all, she thought wryly. She must make a mental note to get the ground cleared and dug over in the winter, not by the arthritic James who normally did the gardening but by someone younger and stronger. Instead, James could supervise the planting next year.

'I wish we had a swimming pool,' Alex sighed when they reached home. 'A lovely, cool swimming pool.'

'Try a cold shower instead,' Sophy suggested wryly, laughing when both children groaned.

This evening the heat was almost oppressive, but there was no sign of any impending storm.

'What are you going to do with Uncle Jon's new clothes?' Alex asked after supper. 'Keep them as a surprise?'

'No, I think I'll just hang them up in his wardrobe ready for him.'

'But what about his old ones?' Alex demanded. 'Are you going to throw them away?' She posed the question with a certain amount of delighted relish.

'Er . . . no, I . . .'

'You could send them all to the cleaners,' David offered practically and knowingly. 'That way he

would have to wear the new ones but he wouldn't
be able to shout because you'd thrown the others
away.'

Slightly startled, Sophy glanced at David's
downbent head. She hadn't even thought he was
listening to their conversation, but he was
obviously far more astute and mature than she had
known.

'Uncle Jon never shouts,' Alex protested loyally.

'No, but he does get angry,' David told her
calmly, 'Not many people know about it, though,
because he just speaks very quietly.'

He was right, Sophy reflected. Jon did go very
quiet when he was angry, and somehow that
controlled softness in his voice was even more
alarming than if he had bellowed at full volume.

'I'm glad Uncle Jon married you and not
Louise,' Alex confided happily to Sophy, leaning
her head affectionately against the latter's knee.

'Don't be silly,' David told his sister scornfully.
'Uncle Jon would never have married Louise.'

'No, he was frightened of her,' Alex confided
naïvely. 'He always used to go ... er ... er ... a
lot more when she was there.'

If it was possible David looked even more
scornful. 'That wasn't because he was frightened
of her, silly,' he told Alex. 'It was because ...' He
went bright red and closed his mouth, an
expression crossing his face that somehow
reminded Sophy of Jon.

'Because what, David?' she pressed, as confused
herself as Alex plainly was.

He wouldn't look at her, scuffing the toe of his
shoe against the worn carpet, eventually muttering,
'Oh, nothing ...'

Wise enough not to press him, Sophy was nevertheless still bewildered. As she got them ready for bed she told herself that it could be nothing more than a little boy's natural desire to protect those closest to him, and David adored his uncle, there was no doubt about that.

CHAPTER FOUR

On Friday morning, after dropping the children off at school, Sophy made her way to Cambridge to do the weekly food shopping. Exhausted by the heat and press of people in the shops she was only too pleased to get back inside her car. The air inside was stifling, and winding down the windows, she drove home.

She was expecting that Jon would ring sometime during the course of the day to tell her what flight he would be on. She had bought smoked salmon for dinner tomorrow because she knew he liked it, and there was a ham in the fridge which she had baked especially the day before. When she got back she would make up his bed ... and perhaps pick some flowers for the sitting room.

Abruptly she shook her head. Their marriage was a business relationship, she reminded herself severely. Jon would be understandably embarrassed if he came home to find she had made a lot of special arrangements to welcome him. But even while she acknowledged the sense of her thinking there was a niggling sense of disappointment as though she had been denied some small pleasure she had been anticipating.

Although it was only eleven o'clock, the heat when she stopped the car on the drive, was enervating. Listlessly she ferried the shopping into the kitchen and put it all away. The cotton T-shirt she was wearing was sticking uncomfortably to her skin, and there were grubby marks on her matching cotton denim skirt where she had touched it with her hands. The pretty, pale blue outfit, so crisp and neat when she went out, now looked tired and limp. She had rolled her hair up into a knot to keep it out of the way and the back of her neck ached from the weight of it and the shopping.

Tiredly she made her way upstairs, going first to the airing cupboard and collecting fresh bedding for Jon's room.

The door was slightly open and with her arms full she had to lean against it to open it wider to get in.

'What . . .?'

She heard the startled exclamation as she stepped into the room and shocked by the total unexpectedness of it she stood stock still, her eyes flying wide open as she clutched the bedding to her.

'Jon?' Her voice sounded rusty and thick, totally unfamiliar . . . as unfamiliar to her as the figure standing beside the bed, she thought wildly, swallowing the lump of tension which seemed to have invaded her throat, totally unable to withdraw her stunned gaze from the body of the man standing in front of her, completely naked apart from the brief white towel wrapped round his hips.

Perhaps it was the whiteness of the towel that made Jon's skin look so brown, she thought hazily, silently observing the healthy sheen on skin that adhered firmly to male muscles. His hair was wet, which must explain why in its damp tousled state and the way it clung to his scalp it should so

suddenly make her aware of the faintly arrogant
masculinity of Jon's features. The blue eyes were
narrowed and watchful but curiously brilliant and
sharp for someone who needed such strong
glasses, the dark hair clinging to his head mirrored
in colour and texture by that which ran diagonally
and vertically along the male planes of his body.

The most curious sensation was washing over
her. She felt so weak that her legs barely seemed
able to support her. With a small moan she
tottered to the bed, sinking down on to it still
clutching the bedding.

'Sophy! Are you all right?'

So it was Jon! No mistaking that pleasantly mild
voice.

'No. Yes ... it's the heat,' she managed
disjointedly, suddenly uncomfortably aware that
the heat of which she spoke came from inside her
body and not from outside. Anxiously she
clutched the linen even closer to her chest,
shamingly aware of the sudden tension in her
nipples. For goodness' sake, she chided herself
mentally, pull yourself together. She had seen men
without their shirts on before—without even as
much as Jon was wearing. At least, she had seen
Chris ... But his body had been nothing like Jon's,
she realised weakly. Nothing like as tautly
masculine. She had never for instance possessed
the slightest desire to reach out and touch Chris,
to see if his skin felt as silkily warm as it looked.

'What are you doing here?' Her voice sounded
breathless and too high. She could see Jon frowning
as she managed to drag her bemused gaze from his
body to his face. Thank God he was short-sighted,
she thought wryly, feeling her face flame for what

she might have betrayed to him if he hadn't been.

'I . . . er . . . got an earlier flight than I intended. Sorry if I shocked you.'

Shocked her? There was nothing but mild vagueness in his voice; nothing to make her feel that he didn't just mean his apology in the sense of having shocked her by his unexpected arrival, and yet . . . She glanced at him covertly and told herself she was imagining things in thinking that he was ascribing her shock as being due to his semi-nude state.

'Here, let me take those from you.' He stepped towards her and instantly she was aware of the clean, soapy smell of his body. Instinctively she shrank back, still clutching the bedding, all too uncomfortably aware that her body was still betrayingly aroused by the sight of him but he was already reaching for the linen in her arms and somehow Sophy found herself relinquishing it. As he moved back, his hand brushed against the curve of her breast and immediately Sophy jumped.

'Sorry about that . . . I can hardly see a damn thing without my glasses.' The words were muffled as he turned away from her.

His back was as brown and well-muscled as his chest, Sophy thought, admiring it and his legs, long and roughened by dark hairs. As she stood up and caught sight of her own reflection in the mirror she decided it was just as well Jon was short-sighted. Where her T-shirt clung to the contours of her breasts it clearly revealed their aroused contours and the firm peaks of her nipples.

'I'll, er . . . I'll come back and make the bed later,' she managed to say as she hurried out of the room and into the protection of her own.

It was only later when she had managed to restore a little of her normal calm, with a cool shower and a change of clothes that she realised she had said nothing to Jon about the changes she had made in his wardrobe.

She found him downstairs making some coffee, and what was more he was wearing the sand coloured stone washed denims she had bought for him in Marks & Spencer.

'Something seems to have happened to my clothes,' he remarked equably when she walked in. 'I don't suppose you happen to know anything about it.'

'Er . . . they're at the cleaners. I thought . . . that is we thought . . . well, with the heatwave continuing, I had to get the children some lighter things and . . .' Her voice petered out uncomfortably as she realised just exactly what she had done.

'You were thoughtful enough to get some for me at the same time,' Jon concluded gently. 'That was very wifely of you.'

'Well if you don't like them, you don't have to . . . that is . . .' Realising that she was gabbling, Sophy forced herself to stop. What was happening to her? Anyone would think she was frightened of Jon when in actual fact he was the mildest and gentlest man alive.

'I thought those awful hairy suits and ancient cords were too heavy for this weather,' she told him simply, 'but if you don't like what I got for you they can easily be changed.'

'You're not trying to change me into a male model, by any chance?'

A smile lurked at the corner of his mouth and

taking heart from it, Sophy shook her head, adding impishly, 'Some hope, you're far too big and muscular.'

She wasn't sure which of them looked the more surprised. A deep mortifying burn of colour spread over her skin but fortunately Jon seemed to be oblivious to it. He had turned away from her to watch the coffee filtering. He was probably as embarrassed as she was herself, she thought wryly, and wondered why she should find that thought so dismal. What did she want? For Jon to do something macho like take her in his arms and let her see how well her description matched reality? Jon wasn't like that. He wasn't interested in her, or any other woman, sexually. She knew that.

'I'm tired . . . I think I must be suffering from jet lag. I think I'll go out and have a sleep in the garden.'

Did he want to sleep or was he simply wanting to escape from her company? Sophy wondered, watching him wander outside. Well at least now she could go up and make his bed but when she got upstairs she found that he had made it for himself. She shrugged dismissively. Of course Jon was used to looking after himself . . . or was this a polite way of informing her that he did not expect to find her in his room again?

Moved by some impulse she wasn't ready to define Sophy went into her own room and changed into the bikini Alex had picked out for her. She had already worn it once earlier in the week and that exposure to the sun had turned her skin the colour of clotted cream.

When she got outside Jon was lying sleeping in a deck chair, oblivious to her presence. She tried to settle down; first by stretching her body out on the towel she had brought downstairs with her and then by going back inside to dig out a paperback book to read. It was all useless. A restless nervous energy seemed to possess her body, making it impossible for her to simply lie down and relax. When Jon had been asleep for just over a hour she got up and started on some desultory weeding. The activity helped to soothe her a little but her heartbeat seemed to be much faster than usual, her skin damp with a heat that wasn't entirely due to the sun.

At two o'clock she abandoned her self-imposed task and went back inside, getting out the blender to make lemonade, her hands moving deftly as she did so. Leaving it to cool she used what was left from the jug she had made the previous day to fill two glasses, putting them on a tray and then defiantly carrying it outside to where Jon still slept.

The sun had moved slightly and now slanted across his face, revealing the taut bone structure. The hair flopping on to his forehead looked disarmingly soft and silky. Would it feel like Alex's?

Suddenly aware of what she was doing Sophy snatched back the hand she had extended towards his face and instead placed it firmly on his shoulder, shaking him.

He was awake immediately blinking his eyes slowly as they focused on her. 'I've brought you some lemonade. If you sleep too much now, you won't be able to tonight.' How cross and ungracious she sounded, Sophy thought. What was the matter with her?

Jon reached for his glasses which he had discarded several feet away on the lawn and Sophy bent to retrieve them for him at the same time. It was a small task she had performed more times than she could count but this time, as she handed them to him and watched him put them on, for some reason her body felt as though it were in the grip of a deadly paralysis.

It was impossible for her to move away even when his slightly stunned glance slid over her, taking in the brevity of her bikini. She could almost see him cringing away from her, she thought bitterly, immediately stepping back and retreating to her own towel. Why on earth hadn't she put on something more discreet, covered herself up a little more? If she carried on like this much longer he might begin to think that she was . . . what? Trying to seduce him?

Prickles of heat ran across her skin, her body tense. What a ridiculous thought . . . of course she didn't want that. After all, one of the main reasons she had married him had been to escape from any sort of sexual involvement.

Confused and alarmed by both her thoughts and her feelings Sophy got up and rolled up her towel.

'Had enough?' Jon asked mildly, watching her.

'It's almost time to pick up the children.' It was true, after all. 'I've left all your post on your desk if you want to go through it.'

There, that made her feel better—restored their relationship to its proper footing—reminded her that there was nothing between them other than a business relationship and a certain amount of cool friendship, and that was the way she wanted it, she told herself firmly. She had the children to share her love with . . .

Love! She froze, staring blindly into space. How on earth had that crept into her thoughts?

The sudden touch of Jon's fingers on her bare arm made her jump visibly and swing round. He was standing right behind her, holding his empty lemonade glass, watching her rather uneasily.

'Sorry if I shocked you. I just wanted to say I'll come with you to get the kids.'

'Very well. It won't take me long to shower and get changed.'

For the first time it hit her that she was behaving far from naturally with Jon. She no longer felt completely at ease in his company . . . far from it.

She was as good as her promise, arriving back downstairs again within half an hour, dressed comfortably in a soft, mint green cotton skirt and a pastel-toned, patterned shirt.

Jon had his usual battle clambering into the car. 'Next week we get a new car,' he told her wryly as she drove off, adding, 'Is there any make in particular that appeals to you?'

Sophy shook her head.

'I'm told BMW make a good vehicle,' Jon offered. 'How about them?'

'They're very expensive,' Sophy warned him.

Beside her, Jon shrugged. 'That doesn't matter . . . safety and comfort do.'

'You managed to sort everything out in Nassau, then?' Sophy asked when the silence began pressing painfully on her screaming nerves.

'Yes. Oh, that reminds me . . . Harry Silver, my contact over there, will be coming to stay in

Cambridge soon for a week or so. He and I used to be at university together. I'd like to invite him and his wife over for dinner one night.'

He might just as well be an employer giving his housekeeper her instructions, Sophy thought bitterly, immediately chiding herself for the thought. *She* was the one at fault, she was reacting in a totally unfamiliar and unreasonable way and had been ever since she walked into Jon's room and found him there.

That must be it, she decided, relieved to have hit upon an explanation for her behaviour. It was the shock. The shock of seeing him, a mocking inner voice demanded, or the shock of *how* she had seen him?

'Is anything wrong?'

Sophy bit her lip. So even Jon had noticed her tension. 'No . . . I think it's just this heat,' she gave him a brief smile. 'Sometimes I find it a bit wearing. Unlike you.'

A strange silence followed her last two words, and for some reason Sophy felt constrained to explain them. 'That is . . . you've got such a good tan you must enjoy sunbathing.'

'There were times when I had to wait for them to run certain tests. Lillian was kind enough to take pity on me and let me have the use of her patio and pool whilst I was doing so.'

'Lillian?' Sophy asked sharply, taking her eyes off the road for a second to look at him.

'Harry's assistant,' Jon responded vaguely. 'She had a condominium near the Centre, with a communal pool. It was much more convenient to stay there whilst I was waiting for the results of the tests rather than to go back to my hotel.'

A sensation unlike any other Sophy had experienced in her life was boiling through her; a mixture of anger, resentment and ... jealousy ... she recognised dully. She was jealous of this unknown Lillian, Jon spoke about so easily. Was that why he didn't want *her* in his room because...? Abruptly she brought her careering thoughts to a halt. Why should Jon have reacted any differently to this Lillian than he did to any other woman? What on earth was the matter with her? She was behaving like a jealous wife suspecting her husband of having an affair.

Fortunately they had reached the school and in the excitement of the children greeting Jon she was able to bring herself under some sort of control.

Tea was a light-hearted meal, although she herself took a back-seat in the conversation.

'Uncle Jon looks nice in his new clothes, Sophy,' Alex announced approvingly. 'We got you some in blue because that's the same colour as your eyes,' Alex informed her uncle, dimpling a smile at him, 'and Sophy has sent all your old things to the cleaners.'

The weekend was as hot as the rest of the week had been and they spent most of it in the garden. Sophy was having trouble sleeping. Each day seemed to drain a little more out of her, and yet she was so tensely wound up that she just could not relax. Her whole body was gripped by a peculiar and unfamiliar tension which left her nerves on edge and made her muscles ache. But at least no one else seemed to be aware that anything was wrong with her.

Even worse than her growing inner tension was the compulsion she seemed to have developed to be with Jon, and yet when she was with him, she felt acutely tense, unable to so much as sit down for more than five minutes at a time.

The trouble was, she thought exhaustedly on Sunday afternoon, that while she had suddenly become aware of him as a man, Jon simply did not see her as a woman at all. He would be deeply embarrassed if he knew the reason for the way she occasionally found herself looking at his body. She was embarrassed herself. Embarrassed and annoyed. What was the matter with her? Even with Chris, when she had been deeply in love with him, she had felt no stirring of desire within her to know him as a man.

Perhaps it was simply the fact that Jon was so elusive ... so completely disinterested and un-affected by her that was making her behave like this, she decided, turning over on to her stomach and trying to relax. She could feel the heat of the sun seeping into her skin as she tried to come to terms with the reality of such contrary behaviour. Was that it? Subconsciously did she see Jon as a challenge? Was that what was making her behave so oddly? A desire to arouse within him a male reaction to her as a woman? But why? That was totally against everything she had felt when she first married him.

At last, worn out by her thoughts, she fell into a light sleep.

Someone was touching her skin with the lightest of movements, strong fingers moving against her spine. She moved languorously beneath them, enjoying the slow sweet wave of sensuality rippling through her.

Jon ... Jon was touching her ... caressing her as ...

'That's it, Uncle Jon, you've got him now.'

The breathy whisper close to her ear made her tense and wake up properly, quickly rolling over.

Alex was squatting beside her, Jon bending over her holding one palm cupped.

'You were being explored by a caterpillar,' he told Sophy with a smile. 'We were trying to remove him without disturbing you.'

A caterpillar! It was because of a caterpillar that Jon had touched her? Indignation and disappointment merged sharply within her. For some reason she almost wanted to cry.

'Hey, come on, it's nothing to be frightened of. In fact he's very handsome, look.' Jon extended his cupped palm towards her so that she could admire the furry creature and dutifully she managed to summon a thin grimace, her colour changing suddenly as she remembered how her body had slowly arched beneath what she had thought was his caress. Had he realised? She darted a quick glance at his face but it was mildly unreadable, nothing in the blue eyes to tell her what he might or might not have thought, and for the first time she realised how very, very good Jon was at concealing his thoughts and feelings.

After that it became ever harder for her. For one thing it was no longer possible for her to deny to herself that sexually she was attracted to Jon. That more than that she wanted to touch him and be touched by him in return. She tried to tell herself that she was having these odd fantasies simply because she knew they were impossible and that in that way they allowed her to imagine she was sexually responsive without running the risk of Jon discovering she was not, since he would never be her lover.

What made it worse was that she seemed forever to be bumping into Jon in a semi-nude state. He was working at the house and either he was just coming out of the bathroom clad in nothing more than a brief towel, or he was in the garden, sunbathing in a pair of faded denim shorts that fitted him so snugly they might almost be indecent.

And that was not all. Sophy knew she was challenging his sexuality. Knew it and despised herself for it, and yet seemed unable to do anything about it. She wanted him to react to her as a woman. But why? If he did she knew what the outcome would be. As far as she was concerned sex was something that was painful and humiliating. She was thoroughly confused by herself and what she was doing. Thoroughly and completely.

CHAPTER FIVE

'I'VE got to go into Cambridge today—I don't know when I'll be back, probably later this afternoon.'

They were all having breakfast and Sophy inclined her head in acknowledgement of Jon's remarks. From today she was going to start behaving differently, she told herself. It was pointless trying to attract the attention of a man who had told her that he had no interest in her sex. She had been acting very irresponsibly, and she was lucky that Jon was so completely oblivious to what she had been trying to do, otherwise he would have been very embarrassed.

Jon's taxi was due to arrive while she was taking the children to school, and driving them there she found herself fretting over the fact that she was not at home to see Jon off. That such a small thing should have such a tremendous effect on her, was worrying. She tried to rationalise her behaviour by telling herself she was naturally worried because she knew that Jon was bound to forget some all important something but deep down inside she knew it was not that. She wanted to be there physically, to be with him, she realised on a sudden start of disquiet, not liking the conclusions that went with the realisation.

When she got back, the house felt empty. She performed her normal household chores automatically and then went into the study to check through the morning's post. There was nothing that was particularly urgent but there was a letter with an airmail stamp from Nassau addressed to Jon and marked 'Private and Confidential'. Was it from his friend? Or was it from the woman who had allowed him to use her apartment and pool? She didn't like the sensations stirring deep inside her. She had no right to be jealous of any friendships Jon might form outside their marriage and besides, what was there to be jealous of? She had known when she married Jon what their marriage would be and she had been happy with that knowledge. She had also believed that Jon was as immune from sexual desire as she felt herself to be. And so he was, she told herself firmly, but somehow she couldn't stop herself from thinking that maybe in Nassau he had discovered a woman who could break through his barrier of indifference. The thought made the unpleasant sensations lodged beneath her breastbone, increase. Tension held her body in a vice-like grip, jealousy tormenting her mind with mental pictures of Jon's tanned body entwined with that of some unknown but lithely desirable woman whose face she could not see.

Telling herself that it was the heat that was making her so on edge and prickly, Sophy went upstairs, stripping off her clothes and standing beneath the shower, letting the cool water slide off her over-heated skin.

Only when it was starting to raise goosebumps did she emerge from the water, towelling herself dry briskly. It was too hot to work indoors, and she was too restless to concentrate on anything. She might as well spend what was left of the morning sunbathing, she thought wryly, hunting

through her drawer for her bikini. As she stood up
she caught a glimpse of her nude body in the
mirror. The sun had turned her skin a soft, golden
colour banded by cool white where her bikini had
concealed it from the hot rays. The colour suited
her, she recognised, her attention caught and held
by her own reflection. It was years since she had
looked at her body—really looked at it that was,
perhaps not even since that débâcle with Chris.
Now she studied what she saw, with careful eyes,
noting the slender strength of her shoulders, the
fullness of her breasts tipped with deep coral, the
flatness of her ribcage and the slight swell of her
stomach. She had a woman's body now, not a
girl's, curved and feminine but those curves and
the warm glow of her skin offered a promise the
woman inside could not fulfill. She might look
entirely female and desirable, but she was not, she
reminded herself bitterly, and the desire she felt to
reach out and touch Jon and to be touched by him
in return must surely spring from some con-
tradictory impulse inside her which knew quite
well that it was safe to torment her in this fashion
since there was no question of that desire ever
being fulfilled. No doubt if Jon did make any
attempt to touch her she would recoil from him as
she had done from all the others, fearing his
discovery of the truth about her; that she was just
an empty sham of femininity.

She was supposed to be sunbathing, not
standing here letting herself get morose, she
reminded herself, hurriedly tugging on her bikini
and going downstairs.

The garden was slumbrous with heat, bees
droning drunkenly from flower to flower, heavy

with pollen. Above her the sky was a hot blue arc, the grass beneath her feet was drying out in patches where the sun had burned it. She really ought to do some weeding, she thought, wryly glancing at the untidy beds, but she was too tired. Since Jon came back she hadn't been sleeping very well, something she had refused to admit to herself until now.

She lay on her stomach, pillowing her head in a cushion, and then remembering the small white bank of flesh across her back, reached behind herself and unfastened the ties of her bikini. It was completely private in the garden and she was unlikely to be disturbed.

In her sleep she moved, turning on to her side, and curling her body inwards slightly into a position that was automatically defensive.

Someone was touching her, stroking her skin. Jon! A wave of pleasure shivered through her and she stretched beneath his touch like a cat asking to be stroked, opening her eyes and saying his name with sleepy delight.

Only it wasn't Jon, it was Chris, the expression on his face frighteningly resentful as his fingers tightened round her unprotected breast, squeezing painfully . . . hurting her.

She was instantly and icily cold, shrinking instinctively from him, any thought she had entertained that she might be turning into a sex-starved female ready to welcome any man's caresses dying instantly and completely. The only sensation Chris's touch aroused was one of intense revulsion. Angrily she reached out to push him away, but he was too strong for her, burying his fingers in her hair, and tugging painfully on it as he pushed her back on to the ground.

Somewhere she could hear the sound of a car and struggled harder but all her struggles seemed to do was to inflame him further. She could feel the hot urgency of his breath against her skin, his voice thick and angry as he muttered, 'You bitch . . . you deserve this!' His mouth was on hers, his teeth savaging her tightly closed lips. She could hear footsteps coming towards them, shaking the sun-baked ground so that she could feel the movements against her ear. She tried to push Chris away thankful that they were about to be interrupted but was unprepared for the suddenness with which he released her and stood up. She turned her head, but the sunlight dazzled her for a moment.

'I think you'd better tidy yourself up a bit, darling, your husband's here.'

What an actor Chris was, pretending that she had welcomed his touch when . . . Jon . . . Jon was back! She sat up quickly, struggling with the ties of her bikini.

'Why not let me do that for you?' Chris was actually daring to reach out and touch her.

'Get away from me!' She stood up shakingly, securing the strings, and looked at Jon. He seemed to be studying the progress of a particularly heavy bee.

'Thank heavens you're back. Chris forced himself on me, Jon,' she told him thickly. 'I was asleep and . . .'

'Oh come on, darling, surely you can do better than that?' Chris was jeering now, but she could see the very real hatred in his eyes, and wondered at the cause of it. Why was Chris doing this to her? And then instinctively she knew. He had never forgiven her for her frigidity and now he wanted to punish her for daring to find sexual happiness with someone else.

'I'm sure your husband is nowhere near as stupid as he looks.' He looked tauntingly at Jon, who returned the look with mild curiosity. Grinning at her, Chris walked away from them. Sophy watched him go in complete silence. Hadn't Jon understood what she was telling him?

She heard a car engine fire and then slowly purr down the drive and bitter resentment flooded through her body. It was wrong and unfair that Chris should be able to walk away like that after physically molesting her and humiliating Jon. She took a deep breath and found that she was shaking . . . tense with an anger that had to find an outlet.

'Do you realise that if you hadn't come back when you did he would probably have tried to rape me?' she cried emotionally. 'And you let him just walk away. You . . . for God's sake, Jon, what kind of husband are you?' she demanded thickly.

Had he even heard what she was saying? He appeared to be studying one of the flowers but at last he lifted his head and looked at her in that rather abstracted way of his, glancing away to remove a piece of fluff from his shirt-sleeve before replying.

'The kind who feels that when he discovers his wife in the arms of an old lover, discretion might possibly be the better part of valour,' he told her calmly. 'You must admit that I had no way of knowing whether his embrace was welcome or not, Sophy.'

'But I'm married to *you*,' she pointed out despairingly. God, didn't he even care the smallest bit? Wasn't he the slightest bit jealous or resentful? If she had been the one to walk into that scene . . . if she had discovered him . . .

'Our marriage does not give me the right to assume physical chastity on your part.'

'But you said——' She broke off. What was the use? Jon plainly did not care one way or the other, despite his statement before they were married that he would not expect her to take lovers.

'Always logical and calm, that's you, isn't it, Jon?' she demanded bitterly. 'You're just like one of those damned computers you're so fond of— incapable of any human emotional reaction.'

She pushed past him and ran into the house, going straight up to her room, and flinging herself face down on the bed. She badly wanted to cry, in a way she couldn't remember doing in years. Chris's attack had frightened her, her body ached with the tension that fear had brought, and her breast throbbed where he had hurt her but what hurt far more, was Jon's calm indifference. He had stood there and let Chris insult him and her, and he had said nothing—not even when she had told him that Chris had attacked her. He had looked at her with his face wiped clean of all expression— totally emotionless.

She was his *wife* for heaven's sake. She had a right to expect his protection . . . his . . . his championship. Chris had hurt and frightened her . . . and primitive though it was, she acknowledged that she would have liked to have seen Jon hurt and frighten him in return. Had he believed what Chris had said to him? She swallowed suddenly turning over and staring unseeingly up at the ceiling. Surely not? She had been so caught up in her own feelings, in the shock of listening to Chris's lies, that it had never occurred to her that Jon might believe them, that he might take what had happened at face value.

Did he really think she was that sort of woman? The sort who would break the solemn vows of marriage ... who would allow herself to be involved with a man who was already married, who had once treated her with such contempt? Didn't Jon know her at all?

Tiredly she got up, but instead of going downstairs and apologising to Jon for her outburst and talking to him about what had happened as she knew she should, she showered again, and dressed slowly, too heart-sick to face him. Her apology would have to wait until she was in a calmer frame of mind. As she went downstairs, she heard sounds from the study and guessed that he was working. Well, that gave her an excuse not to interrupt him.

He was still working when she went to fetch the children back from school. For once their energy and chatter gave her no pleasure. She felt drained and deeply unhappy. This was the time when she needed a mother or a sister to talk to, she thought wearily, someone who would understand what she was feeling.

When they got back, an unfamiliar brand new car was parked outside the house. Mentally admiring the sleek lines of the very expensive BMW, Sophy shepherded the children inside the house. The car probably belonged to one of Jon's clients, many of whom were extremely wealthy men and she paused outside the now silent study, reluctant to disturb a business meeting.

The children it seemed had no such qualms and burst in before she could stop them, Alex shouting out, 'We're back, Uncle Jon!'

Reluctantly she followed them to find that Jon was alone in the study. She glanced round it and then looked at him. 'I thought you had someone with you,' she told him. 'There's a car outside.'

'Yes.' For once he looked neither vague nor embarrassed. 'It's yours . . . I bought it for you this morning.'

She had to sit down to get over the shock. Jon had bought that car for her! 'But it's so expensive! Jon. . . .'

'You said we needed a larger car and from what I can discover, this one seems to combine all our requirements. Of course, if you would prefer something else?'

She shook her head. 'No . . . no, of course not.'

'It's ours?' David was wide-eyed with excitement. 'Come on, Alex,' he instructed his sister, 'let's go and have a look at it.'

In the end all four of them went back outside, the children enthusing over the car whilst Sophy admired it in stunned silence. She was pleased to see that it was fitted with rear seat-belts for the children. When she got inside she found it both luxurious and well equipped. At David's insistence they went for a short drive although she was not familiar enough with the car's automatic gears and power steering system to take them very far.

'Jon, it's . . . it's very generous of you,' she said haltingly when they got back. The words seemed to stick in her throat, her earlier accusations lying painfully on her conscience. She wanted desperately to call back those earlier ugly words, but found she could not do so in front of the children, and it still tormented her that Jon might actually have believed Chris's lies.

Supper was an uncomfortable, silent meal; even the children, it seemed, were aware of the tension existing between the two adults. Afterwards, when Sophy was supervising their baths, she was shocked when Alex asked her hesitantly, 'Have you and Uncle Jon quarrelled?'

'No, of course not,' she assured the little girl swiftly. 'Whatever gave you that idea?'

'I'm not sure.' She screwed her eyes up and then said slowly, 'P'haps because at teatime it just felt like you had quarrelled ... all stiff and sharp somehow.'

'Well I promise you we haven't,' Sophy reassured her kissing the curly head, feeling guilty because she was the one responsible for the atmosphere Alex had so accurately described.

She had to apologise to Jon, she acknowledged mentally as she tucked both children up in bed, and kissed them good night. She had been wrong to say the things she had to him and then to flounce off in a huff. After all why should she expect him to ... to behave like a real husband?

She pressed her fingers to her temples which were throbbing with tension and pain. What had she been hoping for when she ran inside like that? That Jon might follow her ... that he might ... What?

Telling herself that there was nothing to be achieved by putting off the evil moment she went back downstairs. Jon was in the study. She knocked briefly and then went in, her eyes immediately going to the letter in front of him, recognising it as the one which had arrived from Nassau that morning.

'This is from Harry Silver,' he told her. 'Confirming his visit. He'll be bringing his wife with him. I thought we might have them here to dinner.'

'Jon, I must talk to you.' How stiff and unnatural her voice sounded. She could see Jon frowning and her heartbeat suddenly increased, thudding nervously into her chest wall. 'I'm sorry,' she said miserably, 'and I owe you an apology . . . I shouldn't have spoken to you the way I did . . . I was wrong.'

'Yes, you were,' he agreed evenly, standing up and coming round the front of the desk. There was a look in his eyes she found hard to recognise, but instinctively she took a step backwards, only to find that Jon was right in front of her. 'Very wrong,' he murmured softly reaching out and pulling her into his arms. 'I'm not a computer, Sophy . . . and I *am* capable of feelings. These feelings.'

His mouth moved on hers with unerring instinct, caressing, arousing . . . seducing her own, she recognised in stunned bewilderment as it parted eagerly responding to the warm exploration of his lips like the thirsty earth soaking up rain. The bruises Chris had inflicted were forgotten, her whole body felt hollow and light, empty of everything but the sensation of Jon's mouth on her own. He was kissing her in a way she had always dreamed of being kissed, she acknowledged hazily, with an expertise and knowledge she had never imagined he would own. Immediately she tensed but Jon wouldn't let her go.

'Oh, no,' he whispered, transferring his mouth from her lips to her ear. 'You don't get out of this so easily, Sophy.' One hand left her body to cup her face, firmly but without the pain Chris had inflicted on her.

He had removed his glasses and this close to, his eyes were unbelievably blue ... not sapphire and not navy but something in between, she thought hazily, unable to tear her own away from them. Jon was still speaking and it took several seconds for her to register the words.

'After all,' he said silkily, 'wasn't it this you wanted when you lashed out at me earlier?'

Instantly she felt sick and shaken. Did he honestly believe that of her; that she had deliberately tried to incite him to ... to this?

She shook her head, the bitter denial bursting from her throat before she could silence it.

For a second he said nothing, then she felt his hold slacken slightly, his eyes shuttered as he released her and stepped slightly away. Immediately she shivered, feeling bereft ... aching for the warmth of his arms around her once more.

'Forgive me.' His voice was harsher than she had ever known it. 'I obviously mistook anger for frustration.'

Frustration? Slowly his meaning dawned and a scarlet wave of anger scalded its way over her skin. Did he actually think she had deliberately tried to incite him to ... to make love to her ... because she was suffering from frustration because he had interrupted her with Chris? That she wanted *him* to finish what Chris had started? The thought made her feel acutely sick and for the second time that day she was bitterly angry with him.

Tears stung her eyes but she refused to let them fall.

'You couldn't be more wrong,' she told him thickly. 'I wasn't lying to you when I said Chris attacked me, and as for thinking I wanted you to ... to finish what he had started. . . .' She swallowed hard on the nausea clutching her stomach. 'You're doing both of us an injustice. I can't think why you married me, Jon, if that's the sort of woman you think I am. I'm tired, Jon,' she told him listlessly as the surge of anger drained away, leaving her feeling exhausted both emotionally and physically. 'I think it must be this hot weather that's making everyone so on edge. I'm going to bed.'

She hesitated by the door, consumed by a totally crazy desire to turn round and go back, to beg him to take her back in his arms and kiss her again but somehow she found the strength to resist it.

Upstairs she was too tired even to start undressing. She caught a glimpse of her reflection in her mirror and stared at her swollen mouth touching it tentatively with her fingertips. When Jon had kissed her she had experienced sensations so totally alien and yet so totally known that she was still shocked by them. But not as shocked as she had been by Jon's assured experience. When she had thought about him kissing her she had imagined his touch would be hesitant, unsure and perhaps rather clumsy but his mouth had moved on hers with wholly masculine authority, subtly demanding, revealing a wealth of experience she had never expected him to have. For a man who

openly expressed a lack of interest in sex Jon had
revealed a totally unexpected degree of expertise.
And she wasn't sure she liked it. Where and with
whom had he gained that expertise? Had he once
perhaps been deeply in love? So deeply in love that
it had made him eschew all further emotional or
physical involvement? She shivered slightly, faintly
disturbed by the discovery than Jon was not what
she had thought him to be ... that there was
obviously much of himself that he kept hidden.
But why had he kissed her?

That was a question to which she could not find
an answer other than perhaps out of male pride
because she had verbally challenged his sexuality.

Yes ... she decided finally, that must be it. Yet
didn't that explanation too, indicate that Jon was
not the totally non-sexual, mild man she had
always believed him to be? Had she simply
deceived herself or had he deliberately deceived her
and if so, why? Why present an image to her that
was, at least partially, false? That was something
she was too tired to even try and analyse.
Tomorrow, she told herself sleepily, as she
prepared for bed, she would try to unravel these
mysteries tomorrow.

In the morning Sophy overslept slightly and, much
to the children's disappointment, opted not to use
the new car to take them to school. After
explaining that she needed to drive it by herself to
get used to it first, she managed to placate them.

She had promised to drive Jon into Cambridge
when she had dropped the children off and had
decided to combine it with a shopping trip.

'We could meet for lunch.' Jon suggested, as she

was parking. 'Unless of course you won't have time.'

Sophy had been dreading being alone with him after what had happened the previous evening but he was his normal mild, calm self, and she had even been able to persuade herself that most of last night's heart searchings had been prompted by nothing more than her own imagination. After all, it was not perhaps surprising that she should enjoy his kiss. She had wanted him to touch her for long enough.

'Er ... no. Lunch would be lovely,' she stammered, realising that Jon was waiting for her response.

'Good.'

The smile he gave her made her heart lurch drunkenly and, for some stupid reason, she simply sat in the car and watched him walk away, unable to take her eyes off his lean, lithe body. He was wearing his new clothes as though he had always worn them and watching the way more than one woman turned to observe his long legged progress down the street, Sophy found herself wishing she had left him to his baggy cords and shapeless shirts. She didn't want other women looking at him, she realised with a sharp pang. She didn't want them admiring the masculine lines of his body, the breadth of his shoulders beneath the fine cotton of his shirt ...

Like someone moving slowly in a dream, she shook her head, trying to disperse it, forcing herself to get out of the car and lock it.

Her shopping didn't take her long, and she was finished in plenty of time to get to the office where she had arranged to meet Jon. So much time in fact that when she found herself studying an attractive lemon sundress in a shop window, she gave in to the temptation to go inside and try it on.

It fitted her perfectly, enhancing the golden gleam of her skin and bringing out the red highlights in her hair. Tiny shoe-string straps tied on her shoulders in provocative bows, a broad, stiffened belt emphasising the narrowness of her waist, before the skirt flared out over a slightly stiffened underskirt.

'It might have been made for you,' the assistant said, truthfully.

'I'll take it . . .' Sophy took a deep breath, 'and I'll keep it on. . . .'

The other girl's eyes twinkled. 'Mmm . . . well I certainly think he'll appreciate it, whoever he is.'

'My husband.' The admission was made almost before she was aware of it and angry colour flooded her skin. Of course she wasn't buying this dress for Jon's benefit! She was buying it because it was cool and she was hot . . . and besides it was time she had some pretty things and . . .

Impatiently she waited for the girl to take her cheque and put her things into a bag, regretting now her impulsive decision to wear the dress but too embarrassed to do anything about it.

She found Jon waiting for her when she got to the office. He opened the door for her and, as the strong midday sunlight fell on his face, she realised he looked tired. Lines of strain harshened the shape of his mouth and for some reason he looked almost unfamiliar; harder, more male. As though she were seeing him properly for the first time Sophy stared at him, confused. He in turn was studying her, looking at her with such an air of open appraisal that the sundress, so pretty and cool in the shop, now seemed somehow provocative and dangerous.

'It's such a hot day I thought we'd eat at the Mill.'

The restaurant he named was on the river and very popular. Sophy doubted that they would be able to get a table but she was anxious to escape the tense atmosphere of the small office. It seemed to be stifling her. It must be the heat, she thought dizzily as they went outside but even in the fresh air the tension remained.

In the narrow streets the heat was like a thick blanket, clogging her throat when she tried to breath. Far too acutely conscious of Jon at her side, she started to walk faster, arriving at the car hot and out of breath. In contrast Jon looked cool and lazily at ease. But was he? Some sixth sense made her study him more closely. A tiny pulse flickered unevenly under his skin. This constraint between them was a new thing, and one she did not know how to handle. Almost overnight Jon had turned from a kind, unthreatening man whom she liked very much and was fond of in a sisterly fashion, into a stranger, for whom her feelings were anything but sisterly.

Her face burned as she remembered his laconic accusation the previous evening. She had goaded him deliberately, she recognised that now. She wanted him to react physically to her comments but not because of Chris. All the feelings she had been fighting so hard to suppress flooded through her as she started the car. Why did she have to discover them now, when it was too late? Why had she not realised before their marriage that she was vulnerable to Jon's attraction? Was it because they were married that she was seeing him in this new light?

The questions buzzed in her tired brain like swarming wasps, making her stall the car and have to restart it, whilst Jon sat silently at her side.

To her surprise he had booked a table for them at the Mill. Not outside where everyone else seemed to be eating but in the dim coolness of the mill itself. Once a working flour mill, the building had been enterprisingly converted into a restaurant some years ago. Recently it had been taken over by a young couple with an enthusiasm for wholesome natural food, which was attractively presented.

Sophy ordered unenthusiastically, knowing that she was far too wrought up to enjoy her meal. Her throat seemed to have closed to an aching tightness, her whole body in the grip of an unfamiliar tension. She wanted to be with Jon and yet she didn't. Being alone with him made her feel nervous and on edge. Something she had never experienced in his company before, but a feeling she was familiar with nevertheless. She had experienced it every time she had dated a man she liked and whom she had thought might help her to overcome the stigma that Chris had labelled her with. It was the utmost stupidity to want Jon physically, she told herself despairingly, and it was not even as though he wanted her.

She managed no more than a few bites of both her first and main courses, refusing a sweet, and playing with her cup of coffee whilst Jon buttered biscuits and helped himself to the Stilton.

Why had she ever thought him clumsy? she

wondered absently, watching the neat methodical movement of his hands. In moments she was totally absorbed in watching him, in wondering what it would be like to feel those long fingers against her skin . . .

'Sophy.'

She looked up, confused by the sudden curling ache in the pit of her stomach, her breath catching suddenly, trapped deep in her lungs as she saw the way he was looking at her.

'Jon?'

'Some boxes are better never opened, Pandora,' he said quietly in answer to her unspoken question, 'but it's too late for going back now.'

Sophy moistened dry lips with the tip of her tongue, dreading what he might be going to say. She had seen in that look they had just exchanged a recognition of the desire he had stirred within her and was ashamed of her own betrayal.

'What do you mean?' She was playing for time, hoping to stall whatever was to come but Jon did not want to play. She could tell that from the way his jaw tensed, his eyes narrowing faintly as he studied her face.

'Isn't it obvious what I mean?' he asked quietly, carefully pushing aside his plate and looking at her. She wanted to look away but it was impossible, some power beyond her own puny strength refused to allow her to drag her gaze away from his. 'I want you dammit, Sophy,' she heard him saying rawly, the words falling around her, splintering through her self-control and shattering it completely, shocking her with their intensity, stunning her into silence with their totally unexpectedness. 'I want you as a man wants a woman, in my arms . . . in my bed. Oh, it's all right, I'm not going to force myself on you. I simply brought you here so that we could discuss this sensibly.'

From somewhere she managed to find her voice, the sound of it raw and husky in her own ears as she stammered helplessly, 'But you don't . . . you aren't like that.'

His mouth twisted with unfamiliar cynicism, his voice very soft and faintly metallic as he told her, 'You're wrong, Sophy, I do . . . and I most certainly am, much as it pains me to admit it. Poor Sophy,' his voice mocked her in its irony, 'how shocked you look, and no wonder . . . but did you really think me so sexless? Oh, I know you don't find me physically appealing but unfortunately a human being's ability to experience desire is not in direct ratio to physical attractiveness. Or is that another truth you find hard to digest? Poor Sophy indeed. How disconcerting all this must be for you. . . . You preferred to see me as more machine than man, I'm afraid but you really only have yourself to blame,' he told her harshly. 'I'm not blind despite these . . .' he touched his glasses, his eyes and mouth hard. 'Whether you're willing to admit it or not, you've been deliberately provoking me recently. Why? Because of Benson?'

Unable to listen to any more, Sophy reacted wholly instinctively and did something she'd never done before in her life. She got up and fled from the room, rushing out to the car before Jon could stop her, quickly starting it and driving off.

It wasn't until she reached home that the full enormity of what she had done actually dawned on her. She had left Jon stranded at the Mill. All because she didn't have the courage to be as open with him as he had been with her and tell him that her recent provocative behaviour had sprung from a mingling of pique and curiosity and had had nothing to do with Chris at all. No, not just pique and curiosity . . . there was desire as well; the same desire that was curling through her body now as she remembered what he had said to her about wanting her.

Suddenly galvanised into action she ran to the 'phone and looked up the number of the Mill, quickly dialling it. It seemed an age before anyone answered. Impatiently she asked for Jon and, after what seemed like an endless wait, was told that he had left.

He must have got a taxi, she reflected guiltily. Why had she reacted like that . . . like a gauche and embarrassed teenager? What on earth could she say to him when he came home?

CHAPTER SIX

ONLY he didn't come home. At least not immediately, and he wasn't back when she returned from collecting the children from school either. She had dialled the office several times without getting a reply and was now beginning to get seriously alarmed ... he had every right to be angry with her but to do this. Where was he?

She had to fib to David and Alex, telling them that he had gone out on business. Fortunately they were too accustomed to his sudden departures and arrivals to question her more closely, because she was sure her anxious expression would not have deceived them for very long if they had.

Supper-time came and went and there was still no sign of him. Sophy stayed up until gone midnight, her mind in total panic. Had he walked out on her? Was he so angry with her that he could not bear to come back? Or had he perhaps taken her sudden flight as an indication that she found his revelations totally repellent ... that she found *him* totally repellent? Biting her lip anxiously she paced the floor, tension seizing her body as she heard a car coming up the drive.

The taxi driver greeted her appearance with a relieved grimace. 'Passed out cold I think he has,' he informed her bluntly.

At first when she looked into the taxi she thought he was right but Jon was conscious, although undeniably drunk. Between them she and the driver managed to get him into the house where he collapsed on to the settee.

The smell of whisky clung to his skin and his breath.

'At least he's not a violent drunk,' the taxi driver comforted her when she went out to pay him. 'Real gentlemanly he was until he passed out.'

Slowly Sophy went back inside. Jon never drank more than the odd glass of spirits or wine; she had never ever seen him like this, nor thought that she would. Had he done this to himself because he wanted her? She ached to tell him the truth ... that she wanted him too, and wished more than ever that she had not rushed off in that silly fashion at lunch time, but she had been shocked and, yes, angry too that he could be so blind about her. It was insulting that he should believe that she could not see beyond his public façade to what lay behind but until very recently she could not, she reminded herself ... until she had married him, until David had made that innocent remark about Louise—in fact, she had never considered him as a sexual human being at all ... so perhaps it was no wonder he had spoken the way he had.

He moaned and she went across to the sofa, reflecting grimly that in the morning he would have an outsize hangover and a stiff neck if she left him where he was ... but how could she move him? She tried and found it impossible and instead made him as comfortable as she could, relief invading her now that he was actually back.

'Why is Uncle Jon sleeping in the sitting-room?'

Alex asked the question innocently at breakfast time.

It was David who replied, eyeing his sister faintly scornfully, as he said. 'It's because he's been drinking. He smells just like Daddy did when he and Mummy had been to a party.'

'Yes but why does that make him sleep downstairs?' Alex persisted, breaking off as the subject of her question came into the kitchen. The blue eyes looked slightly bloodshot, the brown skin faintly sallow.

'Coffee?' Sophy asked quietly.

Jon nodded and then closed his eyes, moaning faintly as he did so. 'What happened?' he demanded wryly, sitting down beside Alex and taking the coffee Sophy poured for him.

'I don't really know. A taxi driver brought you back.'

'Oh, God, yes . . . I bumped into some friends I was at Cambridge with. Which reminds me . . . I think I accepted an invitation to a party for both of us tonight.' He fished in his pocket and produced a scrap of paper with an address scribbled down on it. 'Yes, there it is . . .'

'You haven't had enough partying?' Sophy asked him drily, taking the paper and smoothing it out.

'Mmm . . . but we ought to go. It's someone who's just setting up on his own and he needs my help. If you don't fancy it, I could always go alone.'

Instantly Sophy recognised that she did not want that at all. She wanted to be with him . . . accepted by his friends as his wife.

'No . . . no. It will be a pleasant change.' She

would have to arrange a baby-sitter, but that should not be too difficult. Helen Saunders at the Post Office had a teenage daughter who was trying to save up to buy her first car. Susan was a pleasant, responsible girl, who Sophy knew she could trust with the children.

'Why don't you go upstairs and go back to sleep?' she suggested to Jon, noting his bleary eyes and haggard appearance.

'Mmm . . . sounds like a good idea.'

She watched him go, conscious of an urge to rush after him and go with him to fuss over him as though he were genuinely her husband.

'Poor Uncle Jon, he looks really poorly,' Alex commented sympathetically, finishing her breakfast.

Susan Saunders proved willing to baby-sit, and having arranged to pick her up at eight Sophy went upstairs to study the contents of her wardrobe. She had attended several business cocktail parties with Jon before and knew what to expect. As his secretary she had always worn something business-like and formal but now she was his wife. In the end she selected a simple cream silk shift style dress which had been an impulse buy in London and which had been so hideously expensive she had been too guilty to wear it.

Holding it up against herself she saw how the cream silk emphasised her tan and the silky richness of her hair. The demure front was offset by the deep vee back; the dress would be pleasantly cool on what she suspected was going to be an oppressively hot evening.

Her mind made up, she went back downstairs, not giving in to the temptation to walk into Jon's room and see if he was awake. Sooner or later they were going to have to talk; she was going to have to explain to him that the reason she had fled so abruptly had not been because she was shocked by his disclosures or found them distasteful. Even now she found it hard to grasp that he had made them, that he had told her that he wanted her.

He came downstairs just after lunch, looking worn and tired. 'God, I feel dreadful,' he told her wryly. 'It's a long, long time since I've been in the state I was in last night.' He sat down at the kitchen table and leaned his head back. 'I have the most God-awful headache.'

Silently Sophy produced some Alka Seltzer, watching the face he pulled as he drank it. 'Filthy stuff,' was his only comment before he closed his eyes again.

'Jon, about yesterday.' It had to be said before she lost her courage but the look in his eyes as he opened them immediately silenced her.

'Not now, Sophy,' he said wearily. 'Just leave it, will you? I think I'd better get some fresh air . . .'

He didn't want her to go with him, Sophy could tell that. Was he regretting saying to her what he had? Idly her eyes registered his progress to the door, her senses wondering how she could ever have been ignorant of his masculine appeal; how she could ever have been blind enough to think of him as sexless . . .? A quiver of heat darted through her as her glance rested briefly on the taut outline of his buttocks and then slithered down the length of his legs. Suddenly it hurt to even breathe; she was terrified he would turn round and see what was in her eyes. She reached clumsily for her mug of coffee, her whole body shaking. So this was desire, this fierce, hot need that pushed aside everything that stood in its path; that demanded and aroused. Jon wanted her, he had said so and it ought to be the simplest thing in the world simply to go to him and tell him that she wanted him too, only it wasn't.

'Come and show me when you've got your dress on.' Alex was in the sitting room with Susan and David, and Sophy smiled and nodded. Jon was already upstairs getting ready but she had only just arrived back with Susan. According to Jon they were supposed to be at his friend's for nine o'clock. She had showered and put on her make-up before going for Susan but she had not changed into her silk dress.

She had decided to drive the BMW tonight—the first time she had taken it out with a passenger, although Jon was the most uncritical of men when it came to being driven.

She almost collided with him at the top of the stairs, his hands coming out to steady her, touching her briefly, making heat sheet through her body.

How on earth had she ever considered him unattractive, she wondered achingly. His hair was still slightly damp and curled into his neck, the white silk shirt he was wearing clinging to his skin. The black pants weren't ones she could ever remember seeing before and then she realised it was part of a dinner suit and that he was carrying the jacket—a new dinner suit, she was sure. He was even wearing a bow tie, and as he moved past her she caught an elusive hint of some masculine cologne, faintly old fashioned and citrusy.

'I shan't be long,' she told him. 'I've only got to put on my dress and do my hair.'

Once it was on she wasn't sure if the cream silk had been a good idea. She had forgotten that the back was so low that it was impossible to wear a bra under it and the silk, almost perfectly decorous, seemed to hint at the shape of her breasts in a way she found unfamiliar. Her hair she left loose, sliding her feet into cream high-heeled sandals that made her taller than ever. For the first time in her life she was not ashamed or embarrassed by her height. Even in these heels she was nowhere near as tall as Jon. She picked up her bag and went downstairs.

'Wow . . . you both look smashing!' Alex told her, her admiring eyes going from Jon to Sophy in excited wonder. Susan grinned at her and then blushed bright red as she looked at Jon. A sharp knifing feeling that Sophy recognised as jealousy tore through her. She was jealous! Jealous of an eighteen-year-old . . . just because that eighteen-year-old had recognised instantly what she herself had been blind to for so long. Jon was an extremely attractive and desirable man!

'We shan't be back late.' Instead of being reassuring her voice sounded slighly brittle. She saw Jon frown as they went outside.

'Are you all right?' he asked her quietly. 'You seem on edge.'

'It's the heat.' It was partially true after all. Surely he knew the reason she was so on edge? He touched her arm as he opened the car door for her and she flinched, red hot darts of sensation destroying her composure.

'For God's sake, Sophy.' His voice was harsh against her ear. 'What the hell do you think I'm going to do? Give in to my animal passions and take you here in full view of the kids?'

He had managed to subdue the harshness to a laconic drawl which infused the words with a certain dry mockery, but they still made her shake with reaction. 'I'm sorry that you find the knowledge that I'm a fully functioning sexual being so distressing, but as I've already told you . . . you have nothing to fear.'

'I know that.'

'You do?' His mouth twisted in a way she was coming to know. 'Then you've a pretty odd way of showing it.'

He walked round to the passenger door of the car, which she unlocked for him, and got in beside her.

She had lost count of the thousands of times she must have driven him and yet tonight his presence beside her in the close confines of the car disturbed her. She was acutely conscious of the lean sprawl of his legs . . . of the rise and fall of his chest, and the cool scent of his cologne mingling with a different, more basic scent which her senses responded to on a deeper, primitive level.

She wanted him, she realised despairingly, and she would give anything not to be going to this party tonight but to be alone with him so that they could talk. Instead she forced herself to concentrate on her driving, absently noting the easy way in which the big car responded to her touch. It was a pleasure to drive, but right now she was hardly in a mood to appreciate that fact.

It was ten-past-nine when she pulled up in the

drive to Jon's friend's house. A mock Tudor building in an avenue of similar houses, it was an easily recognisable symbol of success.

She walked with Jon to the front door.

A small brunette opened it to them, smiling ravishingly at Jon, and exclaiming, 'Darling, you made it!' She giggled. 'After last night we weren't sure if you'd remember.' She took her time before looking at Sophy.

'So this is your wife? Please come in. You can't know how thrilled we were to bump into Jon last night in Cambridge.' She chattered on as she led them through the house to a long terrace at the back where the rich aromas of barbecued meat mingled with the heat of the evening. 'It's simply ages since we last saw him. Roy, my husband, was so pleased ... he's having trouble with this new computer of his and if anyone can help him it will be Jon. How long have you been married?'

She was still talking to Sophy but it was Jon who answered, his expression unreadable as he drawled, 'Not very long ... not long enough, in fact.'

Sophy could feel the brown eyes darting speculatively from Jon's face to her own. In time she might quite get to like this petite brunette but at the moment she was too uncomfortably aware of her speculation and her interest in Jon. My God, she thought despairingly, what was she turning into? A woman who was jealous of every mere look her husband received from other women? She must be going mad, suffering from some sort of sickness brought on by the heat. Or perhaps that frustration Jon had accused her of not so very long ago?

'There's an old friend here of yours that you

simply must meet, darling.' Their hostess was
talking to Jon now, holding on to his arm in a way
that made Sophy's fingers curl into tiny talons.

'Roy, over here a minute, darling,' she called to
her husband, and Sophy watched the burly fair-
haired man detach himself from a small group.

He looked older than Jon although Sophy
recognised that they must be around the same age,
clever hazel eyes studying her gravely as he shook
her hand.

'So you are Jon's wife? You're a lucky man,
Jon, she's lovely.'

'Hey enough of that,' Andrea threatened lightly,
punching him on the arm. 'Just remember you are
married to me . . .'

'Ah, you're jealous.' They were simply playing a
game . . . but Jon could have said the same words
to her and they would have been all too true.

'I think you'll find you know most of the people
here,' Roy was saying to Jon. 'What can I get you
to drink?'

'Get him a drink later, love,' Andrea interrupted.
'Jon, there's a very special friend of yours here
tonight. An old flame,' she added, winking at
Sophy, as though to show it was still a game but
Sophy could feel herself tense. Jon had tensed too,
his jaw hardening fractionally, his eyes closing
slightly, such minor changes, that she suspected
only she was aware of what they portended.

'Oh . . .?' He wasn't giving anything away in his
voice either, Sophy recognised, watching him
frown in the hesitant mild manner she had once
thought typified the man himself and which she
was now coming to know was simply a form of
camouflage. What was Jon protecting himself

from? Her mouth felt dry, her body tensing almost to the point of pain.

'Yes . . . Lorraine. You must remember her, Jon. Heavens, you and she were an item for a couple of terms at least. She used to be absolutely crazy about you.'

'But Jon managed to resist all her wiles, didn't you, my friend?' Roy was chuckling, ignoring his wife's frown. 'Just as well too, otherwise Lorraine would have had you neatly trapped in matrimony and then I would never have been able to meet this lovely lady.' He kissed Sophy's fingers gallantly as he spoke.

'We were all a little in love with Jon when he was at university,' Andrea told Sophy with a small smile. 'He was so different from the other under-grads, far more sophisticated and just that little bit withdrawn. It made him seem very exciting and out of reach . . . challengingly so, I'm afraid. We used to chase after him quite unfairly. All you wanted to do was to be left alone to get on with your work, didn't you, darling?' she added to Jon.

Roy laughed. 'Says you,' he teased his wife. 'How do you think he got that jaded, world-weary air you found so tantalising in the first place? It certainly wasn't by sitting up burning the midnight oil over his books!'

Jon looked distinctly uncomfortable. He tugged at his bow tie as though it were strangling him, but this time Sophy was not deceived. He was not really embarrassed. He was simply pretending he was. If she looked at his eyes, they were cool and faintly aloof, not embarrassed at all.

'Well you must come and say hello to Lorraine

or she'll never forgive me,' Andrea insisted, drawing Jon away from Roy and Sophy.

Silently, Sophy watched them go.

'You mustn't mind my wife.' Roy sounded kind and faintly uncomfortable. 'She's right when she said that most of the girls in our crowd had a thing about Jon. Poor guy, he was forced to live like a hermit in the end, just to get rid of them. In those days girls had just discovered sex,' he told Sophy with a grin. 'It was a difficult time for us men, being the pursued instead of the pursuers.'

'I'm sure,' Sophy agreed copying his bantering mood. 'It must have been hell.'

Roy was easy to talk to but that didn't stop her glance following Jon's dark head, watching it bend towards the blonde woman he had stopped beside. Andrea drifted off and left them, Roy was still talking and she must have been making the right responses but inside she was tormented by jealousy. What were they saying? Was this perhaps the one love of Jon's life? She ached to be with them; to hear what was being said, and was given her chance when someone else came up to talk to Roy. She walked unsteadily away, moving towards Jon. He turned as she reached him, surprise and something else—anger perhaps—flickering across his face.

'Lorraine, this is my wife, Sophy.'

There was no mistaking the expression in the other woman's eyes, it was vitriolic. So much so that Sophy found herself taking a step backwards.

'I think I see Peter Lewis over there. I'd like to introduce you to him, Sophy.' Skilfully Jon drew her away from Lorraine, leaving Sophy wondering if what they had been saying before she arrived was something for their own ears alone.

At eleven she began to feel tired. Jon was locked in conversation with Roy in the latter's study, so Andrea had told her. Although everyone seemed friendly, Sophy was disinclined to talk. She wanted to go home. She wanted to be alone with Jon.

'Deserted you already, has he?'

She recognised Lorraine's metallic voice instantly, turning to face the older woman.

'So Jon has finally married! My dear, how on earth did you manage it?' She laughed when she saw Sophy's face tighten. 'Oh come on. I know him, Jon may look like an extraordinarily attractive member of the male species but looks are all there is. Sexually he's a disaster area—I should know, I spent months trying to get him into bed with me when we were at university together and when I did . . . God, what a non-event!'

Why was Lorraine telling her all this? Sophy wondered, listening to her.

The glossy red lips curled in open mockery. 'Oh, come on . . . you must know it's true. I know quite well that Jon's been living like a monk since he left Cambridge. He always did have a hang-up about sex, and you *must* be aware of it, unless, of course, you haven't actually been lovers.'

Sophy felt acutely sick. She knew what Lorraine was doing now. The woman hated Jon, Sophy could see that hatred shining in her eyes but she couldn't know the truth, Sophy told herself, she was simply probing, looking for a weak spot in Jon's armour, trying to find a way to humiliate him, as perhaps, Jon had once humiliated her. Illuminatingly she wondered if she had possibly hit on the truth. Could Lorraine, like Louise, have been

one of those women who had thought to seduce Jon
and found the task impossible? She looked at the
blonde, noting the hard eyes and arrogant pose.
Lorraine was attractive, there was no denying that.
At twenty-one or two she would have been
beautiful ... and probably even more arrogant,
certainly arrogant enough to swear vengeance
against any man foolish enough to reject her.

She managed a slight frown. 'I'm sorry,' she
began apologetically, 'but——'

'Oh, come on, my dear,' Lorraine interrupted
her impatiently. 'Don't give me that, I know Jon
hasn't changed. He was sexless at twenty-two and
he's sexless now.'

'I'm afraid you're quite wrong.' Suddenly,
soaringly she felt gloriously strong, glad to do
something for Jon ... to protect him from this
woman's malice. She even managed to smile freely
for the first time that evening. 'I can't speak for
Jon's past, of course,' she shrugged delicately, 'but
I can certainly tell you that as his wife I have no
complaints.'

'But then maybe, darling, you aren't his wife ...
at least not in the way that really counts.'

Heavens, Lorraine was persistent—and thick
skinned—Sophy thought wryly, but she was not
going to let her get the better of their exchange.

'You mean you don't think we've made love?'
Sophy raised her eyebrows and laughed openly.
'Oh, but we have.' She allowed her voice to
become soft and dreamy, watching Lorraine's
mouth harden and the colour leave her skin.

'I don't believe you.' Her voice was harsh, and
for a moment Sophy felt sorry for her but then she
remembered what Lorraine was trying to do to Jon.

'Then I shall have to make you,' she said quietly. 'What is it you want to hear, Lorraine? How Jon makes me feel when he touches me? How I feel when I touch him? Those are very intimate details to discuss with a stranger but what I can tell you is that in his arms I feel more of a woman than I've ever felt before in my life. Under his touch my body burns and aches for his possession. I would have gone willingly to his bed, marriage or no marriage. When his body possesses mine ...' She caught the faintly strangled gasp the other woman made as she stepped back, raising her hands as though Sophy's words were blows, retreating to the other side of the patio to glare at her with patent venom.

'Sophy ...'

She swing round, going pale as she found Jon standing behind her. How long had he been there? Had he heard? She swallowed tensely and looked at him but he was looking the other way.

'If you don't mind I'd like to leave. This headache ...'

Relief flooded through her. Of course he hadn't overheard! Hot colour scorched her skin as she remembered what she'd said. Now that it was over she felt weak and trembly. There was nothing she wanted more than to leave, and she went mutely with Jon as he sought out their host and hostess.

They drove back in silence, Sophy leaving Jon to go upstairs whilst she took Susan home.

Once she got back she didn't linger downstairs herself. She too was tired, drained of all emotion. She paused outside Jon's room, without knowing why, listening to the floorboard creak beneath her foot.

The door was open and she heard him call her name. She went to the door and stood just inside it. He was sitting on the bed, his head in his hands.

'Why did you do it?'

His voice was a faint thread but she still heard it, the blood freezing down her spine as apprehension gripped her.

'Do what?'

She heard him sigh. 'Come on, Sophy, you know quite well what I mean . . . that little scene with Lorraine. I heard it all but both of you were too engrossed in each other to realise I was there. It certainly was a very talented performance on your part,' he added tiredly. '*How* did you do it? By calling up memories of how it was with Benson?'

Sophy could feel the blood draining out of her skin.

'No.' She practically choked on the denial. 'No . . .' she added more quietly, 'I simply used my imagination.'

He wasn't looking at her, but she could feel the tension gripping him. 'What exactly do you mean?'

Suddenly she was tired of fencing . . . of pretending. 'You're the logician, Jon,' she told him wryly, 'Surely you can analyse what I've said and draw your own conclusions. I didn't enjoy Chris's love-making, as a matter of fact. In fact I found it a total turn-off. It was painful . . . and empty. I can assure you that he found me less than satisfactory as well.'

'Really? So why is he still pursuing you?'

'Because he resents the fact that I appear to be enjoying with another man what I did not enjoy with him,' she told him bluntly, 'and he likes causing trouble.'

'You can say that again.' He looked directly at her for the first time, reaching one hand behind his neck to rub away the tension.

'Headache still bad?'

'Mmm . . .'

'I'll massage your neck for you if you like.'

Now why on earth had she said that? Tensely waiting for his repudiation she was stunned when he turned and stretched out on the bed, muttering, 'Thanks, that would be great.'

He had already removed his jacket, but his shirt was still on. Even so, Sophy dared not suggest that he remove it. Instead she leaned down towards him, flexing her fingers. She had learned the basics of massage after a bad fall in her teens when she had injured her leg and had found relief from the pain of it by massaging the tense muscles and it seemed it was a skill that once learned was never lost, although there was a world of difference in having Jon's hot flesh beneath her hands rather than her own.

Almost by instinct she found the hard lumps of acidic matter that denoted tension and started massaging them. She felt Jon tense slightly and then relax, although he said nothing. Time ceased to exist as she concentrated on her task. Jon was breathing slowly now . . . so slowly that she felt sure he must be asleep. She eased gently away, flexing her own body.

'Don't stop.' The slurred words stopped her in mid-movement, her eyes widening as Jon sat up, his fingers tearing impatiently at his shirt buttons until he had them all free. Shrugging out of his shirt he threw it on the floor, flopping back down on the bed. 'That feels good, Sophy,' he told her thickly. 'Do it some more.'

She obeyed him mindlessly, smoothing the sleek skin beneath her fingertips, enveloped in the musky male scent of his body as she bent closer to him, trying to tell herself that what she was doing was something she would have done for anyone.

Only he wasn't anyone. He was Jon . . . and she loved him . . . *loved him?* She tensed, staring blindly into space, waiting for her heart to catch up on its missed beat. Of course she didn't love him. She wanted him, desired him, yes . . . but love? She fought hard but it was no use, she *did* love him.

The knowledge was appalling. How long had she hidden it from herself? How long had she loved him? Days, weeks, months . . . before they were married, even? She shook her head, trying to clear her thoughts, and knowing it was impossible. The shock was too great.

'What's wrong?'

She withdrew as Jon sat up, backing away from him. He wasn't wearing his glasses but he was looking at her as though he could read every expression on her face.

'I want you.' He said it softly, reaching for her before she could move, fastening his fingers round her wrists and tugging her towards him until her progress was impeded by the edge of the bed. 'Was it true what you told me about Benson?'

'That he was the first man to discover that I was frigid, do you mean?' She was glad that he had reminded her of reality because it gave her something to fight with.

'Is that what you are?' He tugged on her wrists again, not very gently this time, laughing at her as she overbalanced and fell on the bed in an ungainly heap. She tried to roll away from him, her angry protest smothered by the heat of his mouth as it imprisoned her own.

Heat, searing and intense, beat through her in fierce waves, a heat that had nothing to do with the hot summer night outside. This heat was generated within herself, a blazing conflagration that threatened to totally destroy her. She had never, ever felt like this before. It frightened her that she should now.

Every instinct she had told her she must escape before Jon discovered for himself the humiliating truth but although his grip on her, now was only light somehow it was impossible to drag her mouth from his, to give up the aching pleasure of the way his mouth moved on hers aroused. His tongue touched her lips and they parted, admitting him to the moist sweetness beyond, the breath catching in her throat as the intimacy of his kiss engulfed her and she clung helplessly to his shoulders, aware of the hot sleekness of his skin beneath her fingers; aware of the frantic thudding of her heart against her ribs . . . of the slow ache coiling through her lower body, the moist heat between her thighs.

Suddenly it was impossible to resist. Her tongue touched his, tentatively at first and then more daringly, her body melting with heat as she heard his fiercely indrawn breath and felt the muscles of his chest compress.

Her whole body was aching with desire for him and he had only kissed her. Only kissed her, that was all. Her lips clung despairingly to his as she felt their pressure ease and she thought she felt him smile as his mouth moved slowly over her skin, exploring the shape of her face, his breath warm against her ear.

'Let me take this off.'

She felt his fingers touch the single fastening that held her dress on and reacted instinctively, her body tensing, as she begged, 'Please don't do this, Jon.'

But it was too late and anyway he wasn't listening to her. His eyes were fastened on the twin peaks of her breasts, fully exposed to him now that their covering of silk had slithered away. Transfixed, she watched as his head bent slowly towards her breasts, remembering on a sudden wave of revulsion how Chris had bitten her tender flesh and how she had recoiled from him in pain and shock. Until now she had forgotten that . . . but she had not forgotten his anger and contempt.

She reached out protestingly, her fingers digging into Jon's shoulder. Her voice thick with anguish as she pleaded, 'Please . . .'

The downward movement of his head stilled and he looked at her. 'What is it?' he asked her softly.

Not even the familiar sound of his voice could calm her. 'I don't like it,' she heard herself whimpering. 'It hurts . . .'

She saw his eyes darken and tensed in expectation of the same angry contempt Chris had shown her but instead he said gratingly, 'Is that what he did, Sophy? Did he hurt you?'

She closed her eyes, not daring to reply in case she burst into tears. What was the matter with her? Not so very long ago she had lain awake at night tormented by her aching need for Jon to touch her but now that he was . . .

'Well, I promise you I won't.'

She could feel the tension in his body as his hands

cupped her breast. Despite herself she shivered slightly. He was looking at her, forcing her to meet his gaze, and then he bent his head and gently kissed each coral nipple with warm lips.

A shuddering sigh was wrenched from deep within her, the fear flooding out of her, pushed by the slow tide of desire coming in its wake. The sensation of Jon's mouth against her breast had been both reassuring and tormenting. She wanted more than the light brush of his lips against her skin, she realised achingly. Much, much more— but Jon was already moving away from her.

Reacting instinctively, she reached towards him curling her fingers into his hair, feeling the unmistakable hardening of her nipples beneath the heat of the sharp breath he expelled.

'Sophy.' He said her name roughly, warningly but she was past heeding him, her own voice taut with longing as she moaned softly. 'Jon, please . . .'

'Please what?' His voice was thick and slurred as though the words were unfamiliar to him, one hand cupping her breast, the other drawing her down against his mouth as he muttered against her skin, 'Please this?' and his mouth moved back to her breast.

For long, long moments, the only noise in the room was the tortured sound of her breathing and the moist movement of his mouth caressing her breast, his tongue moving roughly over the aroused peak of it until she was moaning in wild pleasure.

She ached when he released her but not because he had hurt her.

'Don't be afraid, I'm not going to do anything you don't want.'

She closed her eyes as she felt him move. Couldn't he see that what she was afraid of now was that she *would* want it . . . that in wanting him she would be vulnerable to him and that, like Chris, he would find her lacking and reject her? And that was something she could not endure.

She moved away from him and knew he had registered her withdrawal as he said her name sharply.

'It's late, Jon,' she told him huskily. 'I must go back to my own room.'

For a moment she thought he was going to stop her, and then she heard him sigh.

'Sophy, you know I want you,' he told her tiredly. 'I want you to want me in return, not to be frightened of me. Is it me you're frightened of, or sex in general?'

'A little of both,' she admitted huskily. 'I don't want you to look at me the way Chris looked at me, Jon,' she told him tormentedly. 'Believe me, it's better if I go now. If I stayed I promise you you'd only be disappointed.'

'Is that what he told you?' he asked her roughly. 'That all men would find you disappointing because he did?'

She managed a wry smile. 'I'm not a complete fool, Jon. There have been other men . . . oh, none of them were ever physically intimate with me because sooner or later our relationship always reached the point where it became obvious that I was disappointing them.'

'Are you sure you're not just saying all this because you find me a turn-off?'

'No!' Her denial rang with truth. She reached out and touched his face hesitantly, trying to smile

at him. 'Believe it or not, Jon, I find you extremely
desirable. But can't you see that just makes it so
much harder? Because of that, I'm frightened of
disappointing you.'

She got off the bed before he could say anything
and picked up her dress, hurrying out into the
corridor and into her own room.

CHAPTER SEVEN

SHE woke up during the night, not knowing what had disturbed her, conscious only of some sound alien to those she normally heard.

Her bedroom door opened inwards and she sat up in bed, her eyes widening as she saw Jon walk into her room.

He was wearing pyjama bottoms, dark silk ones, and she tensed as he came over to the bed, wanting him and yet afraid of what that wanting might lead to when he too discovered how useless she was as a woman.

As he reached for the bedclothes, she wriggled away, smothering a tiny gasp of surprise as he slid into bed beside her.

'Jon!'

Her protest was silenced by the warm brush of his fingers against her mouth. 'I can't sleep without you, Sophy,' she heard him saying huskily, as his arms went round her. 'I only want to sleep with you in my arms, that's all.'

Unbelievably he was already falling asleep as his arm drew her back against the warmth of his body. She knew she ought to wake him up and send him back to his own bed but it was good having him lie beside her, his body against her own. Instinctively she snuggled back against him, sighing faintly as his arm curved round her body just under her breasts.

They were married, after all, she reminded

herself as she fell asleep; and there was nothing immoral in them being here together like this. Apart, of course, from the fact that he did not love her, while she . . .

He wanted her though, she thought defiantly. He had told her so and there had been no reason for him to lie. What on earth was it that she had that Lorraine and Louise did not seem to possess? Perhaps he just wasn't keen on blondes, she thought wryly, suppressing a self-mocking smile as sleep stole over her.

She woke up early conscious that something was different, but not sure what it was until she felt the weight of Jon's arm across her body. It was just gone five in the morning. She really ought to wake him and send him back to his own bed. If Alex should wake early and come in for an early morning cuddle as she sometimes did . . .

She tried to wriggle out from under his arm so that she could shake him but instantly it tightened around her, threatening to crush her ribs. She heard him mutter something in his sleep and then move slightly taking her with him so that somehow her legs became tangled up in his.

She knew immediately that he had woken up, even before he murmured her name in husky surprise, the tone of his voice subtly changing as he repeated her name.

'Lovely Sophy,' he murmured against her ear. 'Who would ever have dreamed that I would wake up with you in my arms?' His hand skimmed the shape of her body and she felt him shake slightly as he asked, 'What on earth is this? It feels like something my grandmother might have worn.'

It was in fact a long cotton nightdress which was slightly Victorian in design. Normally she only wore it in winter but last night, for some reason, despite the heat, she had decided to put it on.

'Jon, you really ought to go back to your own bed.' She tried to turn round so that she could look at him, and found she wished she had not as she saw the lazy blue warmth in his eyes as he looked back at her. His jaw was dark and she touched it lightly, her eyes widening at the harsh rasp of his beard against her fingertips.

'You must have to shave twice a day.' Even as she spoke she was conscious of the banality of her comment.

Jon's mouth twitched slightly but his voice was quite grave as he whispered back, 'At least.' His fingers curled round her wrist, transferring hers from his jaw to his mouth. The sensation of his mouth moving against her fingertips was oddly erotic. She could feel herself starting to tremble, a low ache spreading through her stomach as he gently sucked her fingers into his mouth, his free hand stroking down her body to caress her breast.

'Jon . . .'

He released her fingers and pressed his own against her mouth. 'No, don't speak,' he told her softly. 'Don't say anything, Sophy. Not now.' And because suddenly she seemed to have been transported to a dream world where anything was possible and only Jon existed she found it easy to acquiesce, to simply let herself follow where he led and give herself over completely to the voluptuosity of his lovemaking.

She had discovered so much she had not known before about him already and here it seemed was something else she had not known, her body recognising instantly that his touch was that of a man who had once learned and never forgotten how to give the utmost pleasure.

Sighing beneath the seductive stroke of his fingers she let him remove her nightdress crying out softly when the heat of his body touched her own but not with pain, or fear, unless it was the pain of being so close to him and yet not part of him and the fear of losing this pleasure he was giving her almost before it was begun. His pyjamas followed her nightdress on to the floor, his hands drawing her against his body.

'I want you, Sophy.' He murmured the words into her throat, sliding his hands to her hips, holding her bones almost as though he might crush them. She shivered and reached out to touch him, tracing the hard slope of his shoulder, pressing her mouth to his warm skin, gently biting the satin firmness of it until she felt the husky groan move his chest. He had thrown off the duvet and it was light enough for her to see his body. Strong and fully aroused, making her shiver faintly with awareness and desire. It was not the sexual act of possession she feared but her own inability to respond to it; the crushing sense of anti-climax and rejection she knew must surely come when Jon discovered . . .

'What is it?' His voice was gentle, teasing her slightly as he murmured against her ear. 'Surely you have seen a naked man before?'

She hadn't really—at least not as openly as she was seeing him—but it wasn't that that held her spellbound in some sort of motionless trance. She swallowed and turned to meet his eyes. 'Never one

as male as you, Jon,' she told him tremulously . . .
and truthfully, watching his eyes darken and his
mouth curl, as his finger traced the shape of her
mouth.

'That was a highly inflammatory remark,
wouldn't you say?'

She couldn't respond because his mouth was
touching hers, caressing her lips with tormenting
slowness, until she was forced to wind her arms
round his neck and arch her body into his with an
impatient moan of need.

She was aware of his fingers biting deeply into
her upper arms as he held her against him, just as
she was aware of the hard arousal of his body
moving against her own but it was the fiercely
draining pressure of his mouth she was aware of
the most, the heated movement of his tongue as it
sought her own. Desire, sharp and tormenting
twisted in her stomach and she pulled her mouth
free to whisper his name as she drew painful gasps
of air into her lungs.

He was kissing her throat, her shoulders,
nibbling at the tender flesh, trailing tormenting
kisses down over the upper slopes of her breasts
and then the valley between them. Her nipples
were stiff, aching for the warmth of his mouth but
he seemed determined to ignore them. Stifling a
tormented moan, Sophy curled her fingers into his
hair guiding his head to her breast, her body
arching up to his mouth in open supplication.

She felt him shudder and for one agonising
moment thought she had somehow disgusted him,
but even as she tried to pull away his hand cupped
her breast, his mouth hot against her skin as he
muttered into the creamy flesh, 'Sophy . . . Sophy

... this time I can't be gentle.' And then his mouth was tugging urgently on the coral hardness of her nipple, unleashing a cramping, burning ache low down in her stomach, making her sob his name and drag her nails against his skin as she felt the tiny shudders of pleasure radiate through her body.

There was an odd ringing noise in her head ... a distracting sound she did not want to hear, a tormented sound of denial dragged from her throat as Jon abruptly released her.

'The alarm's gone off,' he told her, sitting up slowly. He was breathing so hard she could see the rise and fall of his chest. Sweat clung to his skin. 'Sophy ...?'

Sounds from the next room silenced him. 'Now obviously isn't the time to say all that I want to say to you,' he said wryly. 'I suspect that any minute now you're likely to be invaded.' He reached for his pyjama bottoms pulling them on, his body still openly aroused. 'As soon as we can we're going to have to talk.' He bent briefly and kissed her, just as the door opened and Alex came rushing in.

She stopped abruptly, staring round-eyed at them, demanding curiously, 'What are you doing in here, Uncle Jon?'

'I had a nightmare and your uncle spent the night with me,' Sophy fibbed lightly, giving the little girl a smile.

'Does that mean that you'll always be sleeping together now, like real Mummies and Daddies?' Alex enquired innocently.

Sophy dared not look at Jon. Would he want to sleep with her on a permanent basis ... to make their relationship a physical as well as a legal one?'

'You're not wearing a nightie.' She had forgotten about that, and blushed guiltily. Jon, standing by the bedroom door was laughing and over Alex's head her eyes met his.

'Mummies don't need them when they sleep with Daddies,' he told Alex with a grin, sauntering out into the landing.

Of course it was too much to hope for that Alex would let the subject drop. She was full of it over breakfast, telling David all about it, and Sophy was conscious of a certain slightly adult awareness in David's expression as he looked at her. 'Married people should sleep together,' he told Alex firmly.

Luckily Sophy was able to change the subject before Alex could continue it, reminding the children that they would be having visitors at the weekend.

It was on Friday that Jon's friends arrived from Nassau, and on Saturday evening they were coming round for dinner. Sophy still wasn't sure what she was going to serve. She felt very nervous about meeting them although she told herself there was no reason why she should.

An emergency call from one of his clients meant that Jon had to go out immediately after breakfast. His client's offices were in London and he told Sophy before he left that he might not be back that night. She felt empty and very much alone when he had gone, almost as though a shadow had fallen across her day. If she had doubted that she loved him before, she didn't do so any longer. It took a considerable effort to

rouse herself enough to take the children to school
and once she had done she found herself reluctant
to go back to the empty house. Instead she drove
into Cambridge and spent what was left of the
morning glancing through cookery books in the
library and trying to plan her dinner party menu.

Something simple, she decided ... and something cool. In the end she decided on salmon and
cucumber mousse followed by chicken and
avocado salad with a cheeseboard and homemade
ice-cream to follow. She would have to consult Jon
about the wine. Jon ... it was ridiculous how even
the inward sound of his name had the power to
arouse and alarm her. Why should he want *her*?
She had no way of knowing ... she could only
accept that he did and be thankful for it.

The dining and drawing rooms were not rooms
that they normally used as a family, and Sophy
grimaced faintly over their unappealing appearance. Jon had given her a completely free hand
with the renovation of the house, but the weather
had been so hot that she had not been motivated
into making any changes. Now, with the dinner
party imminent, she wished that she had. There
was nothing wrong with the rooms themselves but
they were furnished with clumsy, sale-room
oddments and badly needed decorating. The only
real improvement she could make was to fill them
with freshly cut flowers and keep the lighting dim,
she decided wryly when she had finished dusting
and vacuuming both rooms on Friday morning.

There had been no 'phone call yet from Jon and
while she was missing him dreadfully she was also
apprehensive about his return. They needed to talk

he had said to her but what did he intend to say? Now that she had admitted to herself that she loved him, it seemed impossible that she had not known the truth before; that fierce jealousy she had felt when Alex had innocently told her about Louise for instance . . . she ought to have known then. But she hadn't wanted to know. She had felt safer simply liking him; safer thinking of him as a non-sexual being. She had never even tried to look beyond the façade he presented to the world, because she had been quite content with that façade.

When he still hadn't returned by midnight on Friday evening Sophy went to bed. She knew where he was working and had she wanted to do so she could have put a call through to him at any time during the day but pride had stopped her. In the past it had always been Jon who rang her to tell her when he was due to return, and she was not going to cause either of them embarrassment by being the one to ring him now. She was painfully aware of what both Roy and Andrea had told her; that in the past Jon had been blatantly pursued by her sex and had apparently not liked it. She had enough intelligence to guess that Lorraine's virulent hatred was more likely to have sprung from Jon's rejection of her than from the lack of skill in bed which she had accused him of— after all hadn't she herself had proof positive that the latter simply was not true?

She shivered slightly beneath the duvet, her bed suddenly far too large and empty without Jon in it but she was not going to be like those others. She was not going to pursue and chase him. That was easy enough to say, she thought tiredly as she gave in to the urge to sleep, but it might be far harder than she envisaged to do.

'When's Uncle Jon coming back?'

They were having breakfast in the kitchen—a leisurely, late breakfast as it was Saturday morning, and once it was over Sophy intended to devote the rest of the morning to preparing for the evening's dinner party.

'I'm not sure.' She responded to Alex's question as calmly as she could. She had been awake since seven o'clock, her ears straining for the sound of the telephone, but so far there had been no call.

Almost as though she had conjured the sound up by wishful thinking, the kitchen 'phone suddenly shrilled.

'I'll get it.' Alex was out of her chair first, running to pick up the receiver.

'Uncle Jon . . . when are you coming back?' She paused and then held out the receiver to Sophy. 'He's leaving now but he wants to speak to you.'

Her hand was shaking slightly as she took the receiver from Alex.

'Hello, Jon.' She hoped her voice sounded calmer to him than it did to her.

'Sorry I couldn't make it back earlier.'

Was she imagining the constraint she thought she heard?

'That's okay. Was the problem more difficult to solve than you expected?'

There was an odd pause and then when Jon did speak his voice was slightly muffled. 'Yes . . . yes, you could say that. I should be back by mid-afternoon.'

After asking her if there had been any urgent

telephone calls he hung up. Now that he had rung she felt worse than she had done before. She felt as though a wall had suddenly sprung up between them, as though for some reason Jon was deliberately setting a distance between them.

The preparatory work for the dinner party kept her fingers busy but left her with not enough to occupy her mind and by the time the mousse was chilling in the fridge and the ice cream was in the freezer, she had managed to convince herself that Jon was bitterly regretting ever having touched her. Everything that Chris had said to her was true. Jon found her just as undesirable as Chris had . . .

She kept herself busy, polishing the old fashioned silver cutlery she found in one of the sideboard drawers, carefully washing china and crystal that she had also discovered tucked away in the sideboard cupboards.

She had bought an expensive white linen tablecloth, deeply trimmed with lace, and Alex who had volunteered to help her with the silver polishing and then with the table, stopped to admire the rich gleam of the green and gold banded dinner service and the sparkle of the heavily cut crystal.

Fresh flowers brightened up the heaviness of the room and decorated the centre of the table. All she really had to do now was to prepare the salads and the chicken.

Alex watched round-eyed while she made the mayonnaise leaving Sophy to reflect that she had after all gained something from her mother, for it was she who had taught Sophy to cook. She recognised now that she had absorbed a good deal of her mother's housewifely skill almost without being aware of it.

At three o'clock Sophy heard a car stop outside. Instantly an explosive mixture of fear and excitement gripped her stomach. Watching Alex's exuberant and totally natural pleasure, she wished for a moment that she too was free to welcome Jon back the way she wanted to but she had to be more circumspect, so she deliberately held back a little washing and then drying her hands, timing her arrival at the front door to coincide with Jon's.

Her first thought was that he looked tired—far more tired than she had seen him looking before, and instinctively she reached out to touch him, withdrawing her hand as though it had been stung as she realised what she was doing.

'You look tired.' The words left her lips before she could stop them.

'I could do with a shower . . . it's no pleasure travelling at the moment—especially in a taxi without air conditioning.' He bent down and picked up the overnight case he had put on the floor. 'I'll go up and get changed.'

'Would you like a drink or something to eat?'

Jon paused at the foot of the stairs and shook his head. 'No . . . I ate before I left.' He took off his glasses and rubbed his eyes. Something he normally only did either when he was tired or when something was bothering him. Her love for him tugged at Sophy's heart. She wanted to go up to him and wrap her arms round him but instinctively she was frightened of being rebuffed.

On Saturday afternoon Sophy made her weekly telephone call to her mother, something which was more a duty than a pleasure, especially when her mother still continued to make slightly disparaging references to Jon. For once though, she seemed uninterested in the subject of her son-in-law, rushing to tell Sophy the moment they had exchanged 'hellos'.

'The most shocking thing has happened—I can hardly believe it. Felicity has left Chris. Poor boy, he is absolutely devastated. He adored her, you know . . . spoilt her really. Of course I've done my best to comfort him. Girls do funny things when they're in her condition but even so . . .'

Sophy listened while her mother poured out a good deal more in the same vein, inwardly thoroughly bored with the whole subject of Chris.

'He may come over and see you,' she told Sophy just as she was hanging up. 'I told him you'd be delighted to see him. After all it's a time like this that he needs his friends.'

'Mother, I wish you hadn't.' Sophy was really angry but there was nothing she could do other than hope that Chris would have the sense to know that her mother was wrong and that Sophy was not likely to welcome him. She had sensed the last time she saw him that he resented the thought that she had found happiness with someone else and she had no wish to play the sympathetic listener to him. Shrugging in mild irritation she went back to her preparations for the meal.

Jon was outside with the children. Soon it would be time to call them in for their tea. She had got them a Walt Disney video to watch while they were having dinner and both of them had promised to be on their best behaviour. Not that they were ever particularly naughty, she thought fondly. Once everything was done she could go upstairs and get ready. Nervous butterflies fluttered in her stomach. She was dreading meeting Jon's friends and being the object of their curiosity.

After all her apprehension about meeting Jon's friends, Sophy discovered that they were a very pleasant, down to earth couple with whom she instantly felt quite at home. Mary-Beth confided to her over the salmon and cucumber mousse that she sometimes felt she must be the world's worst cook and that even her ten-year-old daughter could make a better sponge cake than she did herself. 'And doesn't she just let me know it,' she groaned with a smile.

Their two children, she explained to Sophy, were staying with her parents in North Carolina.

'Harry has so many meetings organised for this trip that it just wasn't worth bringing the kids with us. I can quite happily waste a few days shopping in London but the kids would hate that.'

She followed Sophy out to the kitchen when she went to get the main course, commenting as she walked in, 'Jon says you haven't had much chance to get to grips with the house yet. Of course, you haven't been married very long.'

'No,' Sophy agreed with a grin. 'And if it hadn't been for the fact that the fault on the Nassau computer was relatively non-urgent, we'd have had to put the ceremony off completely.'

Mary-Beth's eyes widened and she protested. 'Oh, didn't Jon tell you—and I thought it was so romantic too but poor Harry was practically foaming at the mouth at the time—Jon refused to come out until after the wedding. He told Harry there was simply no question of him postponing it. Not even if it meant that Nassau would have to look for someone else. I must tell you that I was stunned. Jon's a devoted computer man and always has been as long as I've known him. I was, however, delighted to discover that his work means far less to him than you. Fancy him not telling you.'

'I suppose he didn't want to at the time because he knew it would upset me,' Sophy offered, trying to slow down the hurried racing of her heart-beat. Jon had done that. But why? Their wedding could have been put off . . . and why hadn't he told her?

'He's obviously crazy in love with you,' Mary-Beth continued. 'We could tell that from the way he talked about you when he came to Nassau. Mind you there are some people who can never see a thing.' She lowered her voice slightly. 'One of the women who works on the Nassau project was really smitten with Jon. I told her he was married but she's one of those super-intelligent females who always goes all out for what she wants. You're lucky Jon is the faithful type, I wouldn't be telling you any of this if he weren't,' Mary-Beth assured her frankly. 'To be honest, sometimes Lillian worries me. I don't know what it is . . . a sort of obsessiveness about her somehow, a facility to blot out everything but what's important to her.

'Lillian.' Sophy repeated the name lightly. 'Jon mentioned her to me. He used her pool during his rest periods.'

'Yes . . . I know.' Mary-Beth pulled a wry grimace when she saw Sophy's expression. 'Look, you've got nothing to worry about . . . Jon's crazy about you. He couldn't wait to rush back home.'

Sophy smiled, sensing that the other woman was regretting ever bringing up the subject of Lillian. It was silly to be jealous of the other woman. After all Jon had married *her*; had told her that he desired her. But not that he loved her, she thought achingly . . . and that was what she wanted. She wanted Jon to love her in the same total and complete way she loved him. But despite everything that Mary-Beth had said to the contrary Sophy knew that he did not.

It was gone one o'clock when the Silvers left. Leaving Jon in the drawing room Sophy wandered tiredly into the kitchen and started to attack the washing-up.

'Leave that. I'll do it. You've done more than enough.'

Jon had walked into the kitchen so quietly that she hadn't heard him and now he made her jump, almost dropping the plate she was holding.

'You're exhausted, Sophy.' She caught his frown as he reached out and turned her round, taking the plate from her. 'Go on up . . . I'm still wide-awake. I'll get rid of this lot.'

She wanted to protest that she wanted to stay with him, that they could wash up together, go to bed together but she knew she could not. As she hesitated, still standing within the curve of his arm, she found herself wishing that he would at least kiss her, even if it was only one of the lightly affectionate kisses he gave the children. For a moment she even thought he might. His head bent and then lifted again, and then he was releasing her, gently pushing her in the direction of the door.

She wanted to ask him why he had lied to her

about the urgency of the work in Nassau, but she knew she could not.

Even though she tried to stay awake until she heard Jon come upstairs she fell asleep almost immediately she got into bed, not waking until the alarm went off in the morning.

On the following Tuesday Jon got a 'phone call whilst they were working together in the office. Never a particularly vociferous talker, the brief, monosyllabic curtness of his responses made her lift her head from the correspondence she was studying. It was unlike Jon to sound curt or to look as frowningly involved as he did now.

When he had hung up, she asked automatically, 'Problems?'

For a moment he seemed to hesitate and then he said bleakly, 'Yes . . .' He paused, and stared out of the window, and Sophy had the distinct impression that his mind was a long, long way away. They had never had that talk he had promised and in fact since the weekend she had been intensely conscious of a barrier between them.

'I'm afraid I've got to go to London again. I'll have to leave this afternoon.'

'Will you be gone long?'

He frowned again, and said curtly, 'I have no idea, Sophy.'

His tone chilled her, it was almost as though she had angered him in some way by asking. Could he sense how she felt about him. Was he already resenting the thought of the demands her love might lead her to make on him?

After that she was careful to keep all her

comments to him strictly related to business matters. As soon as they had gone through the post she excused herself, explaining that she wanted to go upstairs and pack for him.

It was strange how being in love with someone could invest even the most mundane of inanimate objects with a special poignancy because they were part of the beloved, Sophy thought, carefully packing Jon's shirts. He was normally very neat in his habits but the shirt he had discarded the previous night lay across a chair and she picked it up, instantly tensing. The scent of Jon's skin clung to the cotton fabric, and she had to fight against a crazy impulse to buy her face in it and absorb that tiny bit of him into herself.

She made them both a light lunch but scarcely touched her now. Jon was not particularly hungry either, she noticed, watching him push his salad round the plate. It struck her then that he had lost weight and even looked faintly gaunt. His expression withdrawn ... brooding almost, as though something—or someone—weighed heavily on his mind.

Had he guessed how she felt? Was he, because of that, regretting that he had married her? He wanted her he had said ... but that wanting had been a physical need not an emotional one. Perhaps that was what he wanted to talk to her about ... to warn her that he could not reciprocate her feelings.

She drove him to the station and waited there until he was on the train. He did not kiss her goodbye, nor did she let him see how much she had wanted him to.

For the children's sake she tried to behave

normally, but she missed him intensely and some sixth sense told her that something was wrong ... that there was something he was concealing from her.

It was Thursday morning before she heard from him. A brief telephone call merely to tell her what train he would be returning on.

'I'll drive into Cambridge and pick you up,' she offered, but he vetoed her offer, saying, 'No, don't bother. I'll have no trouble getting a taxi.'

Hurt and rebuffed, Sophy said nothing, letting him say 'goodbye' and hoping he wouldn't catch the misery in her own voice as she responded to him. At least he would soon be back ... and they could talk. Or at least she hoped they could.

Neither David nor Alex would be home until early evening, as both of them had been invited to a schoolfriend's birthday party and another mother had offered to give them a lift home since she had to pass their house on the way to her own, so if Jon did want to talk to her, today would be an ideal opportunity.

Motivated by an impulse which she told herself she would have been wiser to resist, Sophy spent almost an hour getting ready for Jon's arrival. She put on her yellow sundress and did her face, telling herself as she did so, that all she was likely to achieve was to make Jon feel even more uncomfortable but it was impossible to resist the age-old feminine instinct to make herself as attractive as she could for the man she loved.

When she heard a car coming up the drive, she dropped her mascara wand and brushed her hair feverishly. It was only one o'clock ... and Jon had specifically said that the train didn't reach

Cambridge until one. It was a half an hour drive from Cambridge to the house ... but then of course, it wouldn't be the first time he had got a timetable wrong.

Unable to hide the eagerness in her eyes she rushed downstairs and into the hall, flinging open the front door.

'Well, well, surprise, surprise ... so you *are* pleased to see me after all.'

In dumb dismay Sophy watched as Chris climbed out of the car on the drive and staggered towards her. He had been drinking, she realised nervously, and there was a look in his eyes that made her feel slightly apprehensive.

'I thought you were Jon.' The admission was made before she could check herself, and she cursed herself under her breath as she saw the triumph in his eyes.

'So, all alone, are you?'

She made to shut the front door, but it was too late. Chris was inside, breathing heavily as he glowered at her. 'It's all your fault,' he told her thickly, lurching towards her, and grabbing hold of her arm. 'All of it.'

'Chris ... you've had too much to drink,' Sophy protested. If only she could get him into the kitchen she might be able to sober him up and send him on his way. 'Look, let me make you some coffee.'

'Don't want coffee.' His voice was becoming slurred. 'Revenge ... that's what I want. Ruined my life, that's what you did. Bloody—!' He called her a name that made her wince. 'Frigid bitches like you ought to be destroyed ... because that's what you've done to me. It's your fault Felicity left me. Christ, remembering what it's like touching you is enough to make any man impotent . . .'

Sophy tried not to listen while he hurled further insults at her. Surreptitiously she tried to free herself from his grasp but he suddenly realised what she was trying to do and grabbed hold of her with both hands, shaking her until she thought her neck would break.

'Are you cold in bed with him?' he demanded thickly, suddenly, his eyes narrowing onto her own, glittering with a hatred that suddenly turned her blood to ice water. 'Are you, Sophy?'

She cried out as he shook her again and her head hit the wall with a sickening thud. For a few seconds she thought she was going to faint but then the pain cleared. 'Let me go, Chris,' she pleaded, regretting the words, the instant she saw the satisfaction gleaming in his eyes. How on earth had she ever imagined herself in love with him . . . this apology for a man? He was so weak and immature, so ready to blame others for his own failings. Suddenly she was furiously angry with him, her anger overcoming her earlier fear.

'No woman could be cold in bed with Jon,' she told him truthfully, watching the fury twist his face.

'You're lying to me.' He said it thickly, pushing his face against her own so that she was forced to inhale the sour whisky fumes that clung to his breath. 'Don't make me angry, Sophy,' he warned her. 'You won't like it when I get angry. Felicity didn't,' he added, watching her.

Suddenly Sophy knew that he was threatening her with physical violence and she felt acutely sick. This was the man her mother had wanted her to

marry; had held up to her as perfect husband
material ... this ... this creature who had just
openly boasted to her that he had used violence on
his wife.

Suddenly she was so angry that there was no
room or fear. 'Is that what you like, Chris,' she
sneered, 'hitting women?' She watched his face
contort and was horrified by the violence in him
but knew that to let him see her shock would be to
add to his sense of power over her.

'I think it's time you left, Chris,' she told him
coolly. She saw the indecision flicker in his eyes,
and knew that her controlled manner had
disconcerted him. She could even feel the grip of
his hands relaxing slightly. Pressing home her
advantage, she added, 'Jon will be home soon.'

She knew instantly that she had made a mistake,
the very mention of Jon's name brought forth a
torrent of invective and abuse so foul that she had
to close her ears to it.

'You made a fool of me by marrying him,' he
told her pushing her back against the wall, 'but he
won't want you anymore when he sees what I've
done to you ...'

He must be mentally deranged, Sophy thought
as she tried to fight down her own panic, sensing
that to show it would only be to inflame Chris
even further. Even making allowances for the fact
that he was drunk, his behaviour still hinted at an
instability of temperament that shocked and
frightened her, all the more so for being concealed
so carefully in the past. And yet now she
remembered that he had always had a streak of
cruelty ... always enjoyed hurting people.

She was about to make one last plea to him to

set her free when she heard a car outside. Chris, still mouthing threats and insults at her, apparently had heard nothing, and Sophy prayed that Jon would find them before Chris did anything to hurt her. She didn't even dare move in case Chris realised ... but then she heard a car door slam and saw Chris lift his head.

'Is that him?' he demanded, shaking her. 'Is it ...?' He was starting to drag her towards the kitchen. She had a mental image of the dangerously sharp cooking knives hanging on the wall just by the door and her stomach clenched in mute protest. She mustn't let Chris get in there.

Panic shuddered through her and she reacted instinctively, screaming Jon's name ... hoping her scream would penetrate through the thick front door.

For agonising seconds nothing happened ... and she was terrified he hadn't heard her. Chris was still dragging her towards the kitchen and then blessedly she heard the kitchen door open, and Jon was calling her name. At the same time the front door opened and a burly taxi driver stood there. Jon had obviously heard her cry for help and had instructed the driver to take the front door whilst he took the back.

'In here, guv!'

She heard the driver call out and then the kitchen door burst open and Jon was standing there. She gave a tiny sob of relief and closed her eyes, only to open them again as Chris was thrust away from her.

'It was her fault,' she heard him telling Jon in a faintly whining tone. 'She asked me to come over here. She told me she wanted to see me ... that she wanted me to take her to bed——'

'No! No . . . that isn't true!' She was sobbing the denial, unable to believe what Chris was saying. She saw Jon raise his fist and Chris cringe away and then the taxi driver was in between them. 'Best not do that, guv,' he told Jon warningly. 'Let the law handle it . . . it's always the best way.'

'From a legal point of view maybe, but not from an emotional one,' Jon responded rawly but nevertheless his fist unclenched and though he was not particularly gentle as he hauled Chris well away from her, Sophy saw that he had himself well under control.

It was the taxi driver who rang for the police.

After that Sophy lost touch with what was happening. All of them had to go down to the police station, where she had to give a statement. Jon wasn't allowed to stay with her but she knew she had nothing to hide and managed to keep control of herself long enough to answer the questions.

When at last she was reunited with Jon, she was glad of the protective arm he put round her. It was sheer bliss to simply relax against his chest . . . so solid and safe, after the terror Christ had inflicted upon her.

'Will you be wishing to press charges, sir?'

Jon replied immediately. 'Yes, we will.' He felt Sophy tense and looked down at her. 'I know it won't be very pleasant,' he told her quietly, 'but for the sake of his wife, and any other unfortunate woman who might come in contact with him, I think you should.'

Sophy knew that he was right but more important than that was the recognition that in speaking as he had, he was saying that he

completely believed her version of what had
happened. She had told him about it in the car on
the way to the police station, and he had been so
silent that there had been a moment when she had
actually wondered if he thought that she was the
one who was lying and Chris was telling the truth.

Neither of them spoke about what had
happened on the drive back. When they got inside
Jon detained her, by placing his hand on her arm.

'I think you ought to go upstairs and try to rest.
You're probably still suffering from shock.'

'I can't rest,' she told him honestly, 'I'm far too
wrought up. I was so frightened . . .' she said it
under her breath. She shivered as he said roughly,
'If he had hurt you . . .'

She stopped him, shaking her head, putting her
hand over his in an effort to soothe him. 'But
thanks to you he didn't.' She shivered slightly. 'To
think I never really realised what he was like.' She
paused and then said huskily, dropping her head
so that she wouldn't have to look at him. 'Thanks
for . . . for believing me.'

She heard him swear under his breath, something
he rarely did and her head jerked up. His mouth
was white with strain, his eyes dark with anger.
His hand cupped her jaw, his thumb stroking her
mouth, the unexpected physical contact making
her gulp in air, the raw ache inside her, suddenly
mingling with a heady, delirious sense of release. If
Chris had managed to deceive her so well about
himself, perhaps he had deceived her in other ways
as well. Perhaps she was not as sexually
inadequate as she had always believed. After all,
Chris had never ever made her feel the way Jon
did. She had never ached for Chris the way she

did for Jon, never melted at his lightest touch the way she did with Jon.

'Sophy ...' The husky sound of his voice seemed to come to her from a great distance, almost as great as the distance that lay between them. With a small moan she moved, pressing herself against his body, feeling him tense in surprise and then unbelievably reach for her, taking her in his arms, his mouth hot and urgent on hers. He was kissing her as though he had never touched her before, as though he had starved for the taste and feel of her. She could feel his physical arousal and felt her own body stir in response.

'Sophy ... Sophy.' Even when he had stopped kissing her, Jon didn't seem to be able to let her go or stop saying her name. It must be the release of tension which was causing such an intense reaction in him, she thought hazily, shuddering as his hand touched her body, longing suddenly to be free of the constrictions of her clothes.

Almost as though her desire had communicated itself to him he stepped back from her and then picked her up. She was no tiny little doll but he took the stairs almost effortlessly, shouldering open the door to his bedroom and then turning so that he could use his foot to kick it closed.

'No!' Her protest was an instinctive female denial of the desire she saw glittering in his eyes, but he misinterpreted it, thinking it was him she was denying, and contradicted thickly, 'Yes ...' reiterating, 'yes, Sophy. Yes ...' as he slowly slid her body back down to the floor, keeping her pressed hard against him, so that she was hopelessly aware of every male inch of him.

Never in a thousand lifetimes had she imaged Jon capable of such intensely sensual behaviour and every pulse in her body quickened in response to it. There was no room for fear that she might somehow disappoint him, that was forgotten in the thick clamouring of her blood.

CHAPTER EIGHT

SECONDS, or was it aeons, passed, Sophy wasn't aware of which ... only of the heavy beat of Jon's body into her own, the timeless message of need and desire that passed from flesh to flesh and was returned.

She was dimly conscious of Jon reaching behind her to slide down the zip of her dress, just as she half heard the slithering sound the cotton made as it fell to the floor. All these were peripheral things, barely impinging on what really mattered, on the sensation of Jon's hot flesh pressed against her own as she tugged open his shirt and sighed her pleasure at being able to touch him as he was touching her.

Neither of them spoke. They were too busy touching ... kissing. An urgent, aching impatience swept through her commanding her to actions at once both totally familiar and totally necessary so that nothing short of death could have stopped her from reaching down and fumbling impatiently with Jon's zip.

She felt his chest expand as he drew in his breath and for a moment teetered on the brink of her old insecurities but then his hand was on hers, helping her complete her task, his voice raw and thick with pleasure as she touched the maleness of him.

Then he was pushing her back against the door, muttering hoarse words of pleasure and arousal

149

against her mouth, one hand sliding into her hair, the other curling round her waist as she melted into him . . . greedy for him.

His mouth left hers, long enough for him to groan. 'The bed . . . Sophy, we can't . . .' but he was moving away from her and that blotted out the meaning of his words, leaving behind only the sound and her fear that she was going to lose him, so she arched her body into his, winding her arms round him, grinding her hips into his in instinctive incitement.

'Sophy . . .' She could hear the grating protest in his voice, but could take no need of it. To lose him now would be to die. Her senses clamoured desperately for fulfilment, her body out of her control and obeying a far more primitive command than that of the mind. She wanted him . . . needed him. Not just against her but within her, deep inside her, at that place where her body pulsed and ached.

Moaning feverishly, she ran her hands over his torso, arching her back until her breasts were flattened against his chest, her hips writhing against him in a sensual rhythm they seemed to know by instinct.

'Dear God, Sophy . . .'

She felt the shudder run through him and saw the sweat cling to his skin. She could feel his heart racing and knew with a deep thrill of triumph that he had as little control over his response to her as she had of hers to him . . . less perhaps, she realised as he kissed her fiercely, his tongue eagerly invading her mouth. She could feel the frantic throbbing of his body against her, his weight pressing her back against the door and then suddenly he wrenched his mouth from hers, a harsh, inarticulate sound emerging from his throat. She knew, even without feeling him tug off her briefs that his need could not wait any longer.

She felt him lift her, balancing her weight against him and without having to be told automatically wrapped her legs around him, her hands clinging to his shoulders as she felt the first longed for movement of his body against her own.

Each driving thrust made her shudder with pleasure, her body eager to accommodate him, her muscles supplely responsive to the maleness of him.

Her spine arched her body taut as a bow in mute response to the driving force of him within her, the harsh oddly co-ordinated sound of their breathing an erotic stimulation she hadn't even realised existed.

It was over far too quickly, their bodies escaping the rationale of their minds, moving frantically together, meeting greedily as though they had starved for this frenetic physical union, Sophy thought, as her body trembled in the aftermath of the convulsive climax that had so recently racked her. She could still hear Jon's harsh breathing. She could feel the tension in his locked muscles as he slowly released her, letting her slide her feet back down to the floor. Neither of them spoke ... She didn't honestly think either of them were capable of speaking. Jon arched his back, relieving her of his weight, his arms rigid, his hands against the door either side of her head. He leaned his forehead against his arm, and she could see that his hair at the front was soaked with sweat.

'I shouldn't have done that.' His voice was slow

as though he had difficulty in forming the words. He raised his head and looked at her. 'Did I hurt you?'

She ached, it was true . . . and there had been an edge of violence in their lovemaking but it had been a shared, wanted violence . . . a need in both of them perhaps to work out physically the tensions Chris had caused.

'Only in the nicest possible way,' she told him honestly, checking as she felt him tense.

'You shouldn't say things like that to me. They have a disastrous effect on my self-control . . .' He picked her up, completely surprising her, and carried her over to the bed.

'You lied to me,' he told her pleasantly, watching her eyes.

'I . . .' She was confused and apprehensive, but he didn't give her time to say anything.

'You told me I wouldn't enjoy possessing you . . . that I would find you disappointing.'

Incredibly in the fierce urgency of their coming together she had completely forgotten her old fears, and now her mouth fell open slightly. All at once she felt oddly light-headed—free, she realised giddily—for the first time since she reached womanhood, she was truly free of all fear and inhibition.

They were both sitting on the bed, but Jon got up and pulled off his shirt. While she was completely nude he was still almost fully dressed and she blushed to realise she had been so impatient for him she hadn't even paused to consider that fact before . . .

'What are you doing?'

He paused to smile at her as he pulled off his

trousers. 'I'm getting ready to make love to my wife,' he told her with a smile.

Sophy stared indignantly at him. 'I thought you just did . . .'

The humour died out of his eyes, and suddenly his mouth was grim. 'That wasn't so much making love as satisfying an intense physical need. This is making love.' He turned to her, touching her with gentle fingers, stroking the velvet smoothness of her skin, pushing her down onto the bed and lying beside her, kissing her slowly and thoroughly, until she sighed languorously her body awash with the most deliciously sensual awareness.

Now that the frantic need for haste was gone, she could touch him as she had been longing to do for so long. With her hands . . . and with her lips, delighting in his husky moans of pleasure as she discovered how best she could please him.

He had no need to make such discoveries. He already knew how to please her, she thought shiveringly, as his mouth caressed the hard peaks of her breasts, teasing and stimulating them until she cried out and arched against him.

It was only when his mouth touched the moist heart of her femininity that she tensed, trying desperately to wriggle away from him but his hands slid up under her, holding her hips, pinning her to the bed.

He raised his head and demanded rawly, 'Let me, Sophy. I want to pleasure you. I want to give you all that he never did. Trust me . . .'

She tried to relax, quivering under the slow assault of his tongue, gasping in shock at the sudden surge of pleasure invading her, her restraint completely swept away as Jon took advantage of her involuntary relaxation, his mouth moving delicately against the tender nub of flesh he had so unerringly found, ignoring her frantic protests to him to stop.

Then suddenly she was no longer capable of any form of protest; incapable of anything other than submitting to the waves of pleasure convulsing her body.

Some time later ... she wasn't capable of working out how much, she felt him move to take her in his arms and gently lick away her tears of pleasure. He took her hand and placed it on his body and under his guidance she felt the full male power of him.

It seemed impossible that her body should ache for him already but it did, as though simply by feeling his arousal she herself immediately shared it.

'See,' he murmured into her ear. 'That's what loving you does to me, Sophy.'

She shivered, immeasurably affected by the knowledge that he desired her; that she was capable of arousing such desire within him.

This time there was no urgency ... no haste ... and the slow, almost languorous way he filled her, made her sigh and murmur with delight, her body moving effortlessly to the rhythm he set.

She fell asleep in his arms, conscious of an overwhelming sense of well-being ... of inner peace and a joy so intense, she felt it must radiate from her in a physical aura. She loved him ... and she was already asleep before she remembered that he did not love her.

'Good, I'm glad you're awake. Uncle Jon said we

weren't to wake you.' Sophy opened her eyes slowly. What was she doing in Jon's bed? And then she remembered.

To cover her embarrassment she asked Alex, 'What time is it?'

'Supper-time,' David told her gloomily. 'I'm starving, and all Uncle Jon can cook is beans on toast.'

'That's a lie,' Alex retorted hotly, immediately defending her idol. 'He can do lots of things.'

'Such as?'

Sophy let them argue, closing her eyes and slowly trying to come to terms with what had happened. She and Jon had made love. She shivered lightly and felt tiny beads of sweat spring up on her skin as she remembered exactly how they had made love.

The children's quarrelling suddenly pierced her thoughts and she sat up, clinging to the duvet as she realised that she was still naked.

'Stop it, both of you,' she said firmly. 'I'll get up and come down and make your supper.'

'See what you've done now,' Alex accused her brother, 'Uncle Jon said——'

'What Uncle Jon said was that neither of you were to come in here and wake Sophy up,' that gentleman said drily from the doorway.

None of them had seen him come in. Sophy felt herself flush a brilliant scarlet as he looked at her. Alex, who was looking at her uncle rather guiltily, missed Sophy's reaction but David did not. A little to her surprise he got up off the bed, and taking hold of Alex's hand, said firmly to his sister. 'Come on ... we're going downstairs.'

Sophy didn't want them to leave. She didn't

want to be alone with Jon ... She felt both embarrassed and apprehensive. What must he think of her? Had he guessed that she loved him?

'David, it seems, is growing up,' he murmured lightly as he took the place his nephew had vacated beside her on the bed, elucidating when she looked puzzled. 'He obviously thought we wanted to be alone.'

He bent his head, so that she couldn't see his expression and said slowly, 'Sophy, we have to talk.'

He had said that before but this time the flare of panic inside her was far greater. 'Not now, Jon.' There was a note of pleading in her voice that made him look at her. 'I feel so muzzy,' she told him, fibbing a little. 'Chris, the shock ...'

'Of course.' His voice was completely even but she was conscious of a sudden coolness in his manner, a faint withdrawal from her which, because she was so acutely aware of everything about him, she recognised immediately and which defeated her tenuous self-control. This afternoon both of them had been acting out of character. She couldn't blame him if now he was wishing none of it had ever happened but at least nothing could ever take from her her memories of him as her lover ... and as her lover he had been both demanding and tender. She had memories she would cherish for the rest of her life. But memories would not keep her warm at night when Jon was not there ...

'We'll talk another time, then.' He was getting up, and soon he would be gone.

She forced a brief smile.

'I'll be down shortly.' She saw that he was about to protest and added, 'I won't sleep if I stay in bed

. . . and besides I'd have to go back to my own room.'

She held her breath as she waited for him to contradict her statement and tell her that she was sleeping with him from now on but he didn't and at last she had to expel it, and listen with an aching heart as he said mildly, 'As you wish.'

No doubt he was relieved that she was going back to her own room, she thought bitterly as she showered and then dressed. After all, by making that statement she had saved him the embarrassment of asking her to go back.

We must talk, Jon had said, but they didn't seem to get the opportunity to do so. It was now almost twenty-four hours since he had returned from London, and he had spent almost all of the morning shut in his study.

Sophy had gone in once with a cup of coffee. Jon had been on the 'phone, the conversation he was having abruptly cut short as she walked in, almost as though he did not want her to overhear what he was saying. After that she didn't go in again.

What had happened to that easy friendship that once had existed between them? Did love automatically kill friendship, or was it that friendship was quite simply no longer enough?

She was just about to make lunch when Jon walked into the kitchen and announced that he was going out.

'I'm meeting Harry in Cambridge,' he told her, 'I shan't be very long.'

She offered to drive him in, but he shook his head. 'It's okay, I've already booked a taxi.'

Sophy turned away, hoping he would not see the hurt pain she knew was in her eyes, and she thought she had succeeded until she heard him say raggedly, 'Sophy, I . . .' She turned round and saw the hand he had extended towards her as though he wanted to touch her, fall back to his side, his expression grimly unreadable, as he left his sentence unfinished.

There was such an air of constraint about him that even a complete stranger must have been aware of it, Sophy thought miserably as she watched his taxi drive away. What was causing it? Her? Their relationship?

She had some work to do for Jon—bills to send out and correspondence to attend to, but although her fingers moved deftly enough over the keys of her typewriter, her mind was not really on what she was doing.

When the doorbell rang she started up in surprise, her heart thudding nervously. She was not expecting anyone and after Chris's visit yesterday she felt acutely nervous, her mouth dry and her palms sticky. The bell rang again and she forced herself to get to her feet and walk to the front door.

Keeping the safety catch on, she opened it fractionally.

A tall, dark-haired woman stood there, her back to the door, one high-heeled, sandalled foot tapping imperiously, scarlet nails drumming impatiently against a cream leather shoulder bag.

Water-straight black hair fell to her shoulders in a satin sheet, her arms and legs were deeply tanned and the perfection of her slim body was provocatively revealed in a vibrant red cotton sheath dress that clung to her curves.

As Sophy opened the door, she turned her head, slanting faintly almond-shaped, brown eyes surveying Sophy with arrogant disdain. Her face was as beautifully tanned as her body, her mouth painted the same rich scarlet as her dress. The car she had arrived in was parked across the drive, as though it had been stopped in a hurry.

'You are Jon's wife?'

Sophy felt her heart sink as she caught the challenging ring in the American accented voice.

'Yes. Yes, I am.'

'Good. We have to talk.' She stepped closer to the door, and Sophy automatically released the chain, stepping back.

'I'm afraid I don't know you ...' she began, fascinated as well as slightly repelled by the sneering curl of the full mouth as the other woman mocked.

'I cannot believe that. I'm sure Jon must have mentioned me to you. I am Lillian Banks. Jon and I are lovers.'

Sophy recognised the name immediately but distantly, all her powers of concentration focused on her visitor's final statement.

This was the woman whose pool Jon had used when he was in Nassau. The woman Mary-Beth had described to her as rather unbalanced ... as almost obsessive about Jon.

'Lovers?' Her tongue felt thick and clumsy, making it difficult for her to form the words. 'I ...'

'You are shocked I can see.' Slim shoulders shrugged. 'I knew how it would be but I told Jon it was better that you knew. He is a gentle man and would not wish to cause anyone pain.' She shrugged again. 'He has married you because of his responsibilities of course but from the moment we met both of us knew——'

'You're lying.'

The scarlet mouth smiled.

'Why don't we sit down comfortably and discuss this as adults?'

Sophy could not understand how Mary-Beth could ever have thought of this woman as being anything other than completely self-possessed and in control. Like a robot she found herself leading the way to the sitting-room, doing what she was instructed to do.

'I know this must be a shock to you but these things do happen. Jon and I knew the moment we met. We have so much in common. His work . . . our feelings about so many things. You may not believe this,' she looked sideways at Sophy and then smiled secretively, the almond eyes veiled by thick dark lashes as though she were gloating over something very special and private, 'but it was several days before Jon and I even went to bed together. We had so much to talk about.' She laughed, and then looked at Sophy again, adding softly, 'Of course when we did go to bed, I knew immediately how it would be.' She moistened her lips with her tongue, and Sophy felt acutely sick, imagining that full mouth clinging to Jon's, touching his body.

'But I love him.' She hadn't realised she had said the painful words out loud until she realised that Lillian was looking directly at her, the almond eyes narrowed and almost feral in their hatred.

'Maybe,' Lillian said flatly, 'but Jon does not love you. He loves me. Oh, yes, it is true,' she

continued before Sophy could interrupt. 'Why else
would he invite me to come to England? Why else
would he meet my plane . . . book us both into the
same hotel?' She smiled again, the cold cruelty in
her smile making Sophy feel as though those
scarlet nails had just been raked across her heart,
inflicting wounds that would never heal.

'Oh, it is quite true,' Lillian said softly. 'You
may check if you wish. We were booked into
separate rooms of course. Here, I have the number
of the hotel.' She opened her bag and gave Sophy
a brochure.

'Well . . . are you going to ring them?'

What was the point? Sophy knew she couldn't
be lying. Everything was so clear now. No wonder
Jon had been so off-hand with her . . . so strained
before he went to London. But he had come back.
He had made love to her . . .

'Unfortunately we had a quarrel while we were
there.' She shrugged again. 'Jon wanted me to
come back here with him but I told him he must
tell you about us first. We argued and he left. This
morning though he telephoned me and we made
up . . .'

Suddenly the reason Jon had made love to her was
sickeningly clear to Sophy. He had quarrelled with
Lillian and had made love to her out of nothing
more than sheer physical frustration. She felt sick to
her soul when she thought of how she had responded
to him, how she had felt in his arms . . . but it had not
been her he was loving, it had been this woman
sitting so triumphantly opposite her, watching her
now with hard, cold eyes.

'Why have you come here?' Sophy asked
tonelessly.

'Surely that is obvious? To see Jon and to tell
you that you no longer have any place in his life.
You must understand that Jon and I love one
another, that I am the one he wants at his side.'

'But *I* am the one he married,' Sophy persisted,
not really knowing why she was fighting or what
for; she had already lost it all.

'A piece of paper that means nothing ... Jon
will divorce you.'

What could she say? Part of her could not
believe that any of this was really happening. The
Jon that Lillian was talking about was not the Jon
she knew ... but then what did she really know
about the man she had married? She had thought
him sexless, remote, totally engrossed in his work
and she had discovered for herself that none of
those things were true.

'Of course you will be provided for financially.'

Sophy glanced up at that, her mouth hardening,
but before she could speak her tormentor
continued coolly. 'You will stay here in this house
with the children. Jon will come back to Nassau
with me.'

She would stay with the children? She blinked
and stared at Lillian. 'The children are Jon's
responsibility,' she said coldly. 'They are the son
and daughter of his dead brother.'

For the first time since Lillian's arrival she felt
she was the one with the advantage. Lillian
blinked and frowned, her superb composure
deserting her briefly, her mouth twisting petulantly.

'Jon does not want them,' she said positively at
last. 'All he wants is me.'

Now it was Sophy's turn to frown. That did not

sound like the Jon she knew . . . or at least thought
she knew but then she remembered that before
they had married Jon had mentioned putting the
children in a home. He seemed to love them so
much, though. Just as he seemed to want you so
much, a bitter little voice mocked her, and look
how real that was.

Through the sitting-room window she saw a taxi
come down the drive and stop. Motionlessly she
watched Jon get out, and pause to pay the driver.
He looked tired, she noticed, immediately checking
the pain and anguish that welled up inside her.

From her chair Lillian could not see the
window. Smiling tightly at her Sophy got up.

'Please excuse me a second,' she muttered
moving to open the door. She really could not
endure any more, and certainly not the sight of
Jon being reunited with the woman he loved.

She reached the front door at the same time as
Jon, opening it for him. He started to smile at her,
the smile freezing suddenly, as he demanded,
'What's wrong?'

Sophy was shaking now with a mixture of anger
and agony. How could he stand there and pretend
a concern for her they both knew he could not
possibly feel?

In a voice tight with pain she told him. 'You've
got a visitor—in the sitting-room. Lillian Banks!'
She almost spat the name at him, half of her
knowing that she was reacting like someone in a
soap melodrama, the other half acknowledging
that like any other human being she was
conditioned to react to pain so instinctively that
her responses were bound to appear trite and
theatrical. 'She's just been telling me about your

plans for the future—plans which it seems don't include either me or the children ... Well, that's fine by me,' she rushed on bitterly. 'In fact it's probably the very best thing that could have happened.' It wasn't what she had intended to say at all, but hurt pride compelled her to make some attempt at self-defence; to at least try to hide from Jon the hurt he was causing her.

His hand shot out gripping her wrist, making her cry out sharply in physical pain.

She had never seen him look so hard or so angry before, and she could not understand why he was doing so now. 'Are you trying to tell me you want our marriage to end, Sophy?' he demanded harshly. 'Is that what you're saying?'

'Yes! Yes!' She practically screamed the word at him, tears flooding down her face as she tried desperately to pull away from him. The sitting-room door opened and Lillian exclaimed purringly, 'Jon, darling ...' Sophy felt the pressure round her wrist relax and instinctively made her escape, fleeing upstairs to the privacy and sanctuary of her own bedroom.

Once there, oddly enough, her tears stopped. The pain inside her was too intense for crying. Later she couldn't recall how long she stayed there ... how much time elapsed after Jon's arrival before he left again, this time with Lillian.

From her window Sophy saw them both get into Lillian's car. Lillian was smiling but she couldn't see Jon's face.

So this was how marriages ended, she thought emptily once they had gone. So this was what it felt like to be the victim of a broken marriage. Empty ... alone ... waiting for a pain so enormous and overwhelming that the very thought of it made her shiver in dread.

Somehow she managed to go downstairs and through the motions of making herself a cup of coffee. Somehow she remembered that the children had to be collected from school, that life had to go on as normal.

The 'phone rang. She hesitated before answering it, and then picked up the receiver.

'Sophy?'

She recognised Harry's American accent straight away.

'Is Jon there?' He sounded anxious and flustered.

'He's just left.' How toneless and light her own voice was. She replaced the receiver slowly. The 'phone started to ring again almost immediately, its summons imperative and sharp. She stared at it unblinkingly and then took it off the hook. She had the children to pick up, she must remember that.

Later Sophy realised that she had had no right to be driving at all that afternoon, never mind in such a potentially lethal, powerful car. All her actions were automatic and reflexive, directed by that tiny part of her brain which was not trying desperately to assimilate her pain.

She even managed to smile at David and Alex as they clambered into the car and started chattering to her, although she was conscious of David giving her one or two puzzled looks.

How could Jon not want them? A fierce wave of protective love for them surged over her. Well she would want them and she would fight for the right to love and care for them. Slowly different pieces

of information were filtering through her brain.
She stared at the house as she parked the car. How
could she afford to keep it on? How much of an
allowance would Jon give her? He was a
comparatively wealthy man but her heart rebelled
at the thought of taking so much as a penny from
him. If she wanted to keep the children though,
she would have to support them. She couldn't
work full-time and give them the love and
attention they were going to need. Didn't Jon care
what he was doing to them, even if he didn't care
about her? He owed it to them. She sighed and
tried to redirect her thoughts. She had seen this
same situation played out so often before . . . when
did adults ever really think about their children,
when they were gripped by the intensity of love?
People these days weren't brought up to put others
before themselves any longer and in many ways
that was a good thing. Too many people, mainly
of her own sex, had made themselves martyrs to
others' demands and needs too often in the past . . .
but the children. Stop thinking about it, she told
herself as she went into the house. She knew she
had to stop the tormenting thoughts swirling
round in her mind or go mad from the agony of
them. She tried to submerge them in physical
activity, busying herself making the milkshake the
children always had when they came back from
school.

'When will Uncle Jon be back?' David asked as
he and Alex sat down at the table. Instantly Sophy
stiffened. What should she tell them? For the first
time it struck her that Jon might not come back at
all, ever. The knowledge was like a physical blow,
so painful that she went white.

'Sophy, what's wrong?' There was anxiety and something else in David's voice. Fear?

Resolutely Sophy pulled herself together and tried to smile. Her facial muscles were so stiff she could barely move them.

'Nothing,' she said as reassuringly as she could. 'I'm not sure when he will be back.'

'Where's he gone?'

That was Alex, frowning slightly, picking up the atmosphere of tension that hung over the kitchen. 'Where is he?'

'He had to go out.' Careful, Sophy, she warned herself, any more of this and you'll be breaking down completely. Walking over to the sink so that she had her back to them, she said as carelessly as she could, 'You know what he's like when he's . . . working. I don't really know when he'll be back.'

It seemed to satisfy them, but for how long? Surely Jon wouldn't leave her to tell them alone? But no . . . he wasn't that sort of man. Was he?

CHAPTER NINE

THE 'phone rang at ten o'clock and she knew it was Jon even before she picked up the receiver. It was the call she had been dreading all evening, ever since she had put the receiver in its place after putting the children to bed.

'Sophy?' He said her name roughly, angrily almost and that hurt. By what right was he angry with her? She was the one who should feel that emotion but her pain was too great to allow her the relief of anger.

'Sophy, we need to talk.' Urgency laced the words closely together making his voice sharper, different. Already he was alien to her ... not the Jon she knew but a different Jon.

Jealousy tore at her, making it impossible for her to speak to him without breaking down completely, her 'No!' rough and unsteady.

'Sophy!' He said her name again, and the receiver shook in her damp hand. She knew she did not have the control to go through what had to be gone through right now. She couldn't even listen to the angry cadences of his voice without breaking apart inside, without remembering how he had said her name while they made love ... how the reverberations of it had passed from his body to her own.

'Jon, please. Lillian has told me everything.' She was speaking quickly, lightly as though not daring to linger over the words in case that made them too real. She heard him swear and flinched.

'Sophy . . . please . . .'

'No . . . no. I don't want to talk about it, Jon. Let's just go ahead and get a divorce. I'll stay here with the children.' Her voice petered out as she sensed his shock. 'Unless you want us to move out.' She thought she heard him draw in his breath harshly, a sound of painful anguish as though somehow she had hurt him. Or was it that hearing the words was making it real for him too . . . making him see what he would be doing to David and Alex. The children will stay with you, Lillian had said, we don't want them.

'No! Promise me you won't move out, Sophy. Promise me.'

'Very well . . .'

She heard him sigh as though her soft acquiescence was not enough and then he was saying thickly, 'Have you thought about what this is going to do to the kids, Sophy?'

Had *she* thought about it? All at once she was angry, so much so that she could not speak to him any more. She put down the receiver with a bang and then wiped her damp palm distastefully on her skirt.

The 'phone rang again almost immediately and she stared at it wanting to deny its imperative call, but somehow impelled to pick up the receiver.

'Sophy. No, don't hang up . . . listen to me. If you need to get in touch with me for anything, I'm staying with Harry and Mary-Beth in Cambridge.' As though something in her silence encouraged him he went on raggedly. 'We have to talk, Sophy. We . . .'

It was that 'we' that did it. There was no 'we' where they were concerned. They were not a single unit but two separate ones.

In a cold precise little voice she barely recognised as her own she asked slowly. 'And Lillian, Jon, is she staying with Harry and Mary-Beth too?'

She heard him swear, and then say curtly. 'Yes, she is, but Sophy——'

She cut him off before he could say any more, telling him quietly, 'Then I don't think we have anything to say to one another really, do you, Jon?'

This time, after she had replaced the receiver, the telephone did not ring again and she did not really expect it to.

Upstairs alone in bed, she tried to clear her mind so that she could force it to accept a truth it did not want to know. It hurt that Jon had not even told her himself about Lillian. She had known something was wrong but she had had no idea what that something was.

She laughed then, a high hysterical sound that shocked her own ears until she controlled it. How ironic that Jon should meet and fall in love with Lillian such a very short time after marrying her.

How doubly ironic when she remembered what Mary-Beth had said about Jon postponing the trip so that they could be married first. How he must have regretted not waiting. She turned uneasily in her bed wondering how long it would take their divorce to go through. She wasn't very well up in the legalities of these things. And then her mind drifted to David and Alex. Both of them adored Jon. How could she tell them what was happening in such a way that neither of them would ever know that their uncle had rejected them?

It was all so out of character somehow and yet wasn't she just telling herself that because she didn't want to believe the truth? She had to hand it to Lillian, coming to see her like that. In her place she doubted that she would have had the courage to do so. And yet Sophy knew that Lillian had enjoyed telling her, hurting her. The thought of Jon deliberately lying to her, so that he could be with Lillian, was so galling and painful that she could scarcely endure it. And then to come back and make love to her ... to substitute her for Lillian, because that was surely what he had done.

He said he wanted you, an inner voice taunted her ... perhaps he had, Sophy acknowledged. Man was a strange animal and could desire what he did not love ... or perhaps that had simply been his way of trying to fight free of his love for Lillian. Perhaps he had felt honour bound to at least try to make a success of their marriage and maybe he had hoped that in making love to her he could forget the other woman. Obviously he had not done so.

By the time morning came, she was totally exhausted and had to drag herself downstairs to get the children's breakfast.

Both of them commented on her pale face.

'I haven't been feeling very well,' she fibbed to them and saw David's eyes widen as he asked her curiously, 'Does that mean you and Uncle Jon are going to have a baby? Ladies sometimes aren't very well when they do.'

A baby? She managed a tight smile and shook her head negatively. But what if she was wrong?

What if she was carrying Jon's child? It was, after all, perfectly possible.

She would just have to worry about that eventually if it actually happened, she told herself grimly.

Because it was a Saturday there was no need for her to take the children to school but both of them had made arrangements to see friends and by the time Sophy got back from ferrying them to their individual destinations it was gone eleven o'clock.

As she turned into the drive she realised that the day had become very overcast, the threat of thunder hanging sullenly on the too still air.

It was time the weather broke; they needed a storm to clear the air and rain for the over-parched garden. A tension headache gripped her forehead in a vice as she walked inside. She had always been petrified of storms. Not so much the thunder but the lightning—a childhood hang-up from a story someone had once told her about someone being struck by lightning and 'frizzled to death'. Knowing now that her fear was illogical still did not remove it and she shivered slightly as she made herself a cup of coffee, dreading the storm to come.

The house had never seemed more empty. She had loved it when she first came here as Jon's assistant, and what happy plans she had made for it when she had agreed to marry him. She had pictured it as a proper home ... Now she was alone with the reality that said a house no matter how pleasant was merely a shell. It was people who made that shell a home.

By one o'clock the sky was a sullen grey; and it was dark enough for her to need to switch the kitchen light on. The sudden ring on the front doorbell jarred her too sensitive nerves.

Jon! She whispered the name, trying to control the crazy leap of her pulses and to deny the sudden mental picture she had of the man. How could there ever have been a time when she had scathingly dismissed him as sexually unattractive? Being married to him had been like discovering a completely different person hidden away behind a protective disguise.

In his touch, in his kiss, was all the maleness any woman could ever want, she acknowledged weakly, knowing, even as she fought to subdue the traitorous leap of hope jerking her heart, that it would not be Jon outside. After all why would he ring the bell when he had a key and why would he come back at all, when he had already taken what he really wanted with him?

Nevertheless she went to open the door, her face losing all colour when she saw Mary-Beth standing outside.

'No. Sophy . . . please let me in,' the American woman pleaded, guessing from her expression that Sophy did not want to see her.

Good manners prevented Sophy from shutting the door in her face but her back was rigid with withdrawal as she stepped back into the hall.

'Sophy, Jon doesn't know I'm here,' Mary-Beth began, following her into the kitchen, watching as Sophy tensed as she caught the distant noise of thunder—so distant that Sophy had had to strain her ears to catch it. The storm was still a good way off. She tried to relax. She had no idea what Mary-Beth was doing here, but since she had come . . . She sighed, and asked her guest if she wanted a cup of coffee.

'What I want is for you to sit down and tell me why you've thrown Jon out,' Mary-Beth told her forthrightly. 'I thought you loved him.'

'I do.' The admission was wrung out of her before she could silence it, her face ashen as she realised her idiocy.

Her ears, tensely alert for the sound, caught the still distant dullness roll of fresh thunder.

'Do you find storms frightening?'

She gave Mary-Beth a tense grimace, and acknowledged shortly, 'Yes.' Another time she might have wondered at the faintly pleased gleam she saw in the other woman's eyes but not now.

Her defences completely destroyed by losing Jon, the threat of a thunder storm was just more than she could cope with.

'Sophy, come and sit down.' Very gently Mary-Beth touched her arm, picking up both mugs of coffee and gently shepherding Sophy into the sitting-room.

She waited until they were both sitting down before speaking again and then said quietly, 'I can understand why you feel hurt and angry with Jon for deceiving you but why won't you let him talk to you . . . explain?'

Sophy tried to appear calmer than she felt. 'What is there left to talk about?' she asked emotionlessly. 'I think Lillian has already said it all.' She shrugged and spread her hands, disturbed to see how much they shook. 'She and Jon are lovers . . . Jon wants to divorce me so that he can be with her. It is all quite plain really . . . I don't need telling twice.'

Her voice sharpened with anguish over the last words and she got up, pacing over to the window to stare at the yellow tinged greyness of the overcast sky.

'Lillian told you that she and Jon were *lovers*?'

Why was Mary-Beth sounding so shocked? Jon and Lillian were staying with her. She must be perfectly aware of the situation.

'She told me everything,' Sophy reiterated expressionlessly. 'About how Jon asked her to come to London ... how they stayed there together in an hotel.' Her mouth twisted bitterly. 'She even suggested I should ring the hotel and check.'

'Sophy?'

She swung round to look at Mary-Beth as she caught the anxiety in her voice but the frown on Mary-Beth's face suddenly lifted. 'Oh, it's all right. You will be staying here?'

'If Jon lets me. Lillian told me that they don't want the children and even if I didn't love both of them very much myself, I could hardly walk out and leave them.' She saw Mary-Beth look at her watch and then the American was saying hurriedly, 'Look I must run ... Are you doing anything during the rest of the day? Going out?'

She must be embarrassed, Sophy realised, and that was why she was having to take refuge in inane social chit-chat; even so she responded to the questions, shaking her head and explaining that both children were out with friends and would not be back until after supper.

Thunder rolled again, marginally nearer this time and Sophy winced.

'If I were you I'd go upstairs and bury your head under a pillow,' Mary-Beth suggested. 'That way you won't hear it.'

Sophy walked with her to the door and watched until her car had completely disappeared feeling that somehow she had just severed her final link with Jon. The ache in her temples had become a fully fledged pain; pain, in fact, seemed to invade her whole body. She went upstairs on dragging feet but instead of going into her own room she went into Jon's.

The room was clean and tidy just as she had left it after cleaning it yesterday morning and yet overwhelmingly it reminded her of him. One of his shirts half hung out of the laundry basket by the door and she went automatically to push it in, tensing as her fingers curled round the soft cotton and she was irresistibly aware of how the fabric had clung to his body. Like a sleepwalker she lifted the shirt from the empty basket, pressing its softness to her face. She wanted to cry but the tears had solidified in a lump in her chest—a lump that ached and hurt with every breath she tried to take. A scent that was exclusively Jon's filled her senses with an awareness of him and almost without realising what she was doing she stumbled over to his bed and flung herself down full length on it, still clutching his shirt. Outside the sky darkened, suddenly split by the first sizzling arc of lightning. Sophy cried out curling up into a tense ball, burying her face in Jon's pillow.

Her fear of the storm seemed to release the tight knot of pain inside her and suddenly she was crying, tearing, ugly sobs that shook her body and soaked the shirt and pillow she was still clinging to. Outside the storm drew nearer and her tears slowly gave way to terror. Logic told her that she should get up and close the curtains but the fear chaining her to the bed was too great.

An hour, maybe more, passed as she lay there too terrified to move and yet oddly comforted by the indefinable presence of Jon that still clung to the room.

Suddenly it started to rain, almost torrentially so, the sound of it drowning out everything else.

Downstairs a door banged and Sophy listened to it, wondering if she had left a window open. If so the floor beneath it would surely be soaked.

Closer now the thunder rolled, lightning arcing brilliantly across the sky, illuminating the darkness of the room. She moaned and covered her ears.

'Sophy.'

A hand touched her shoulder. Her eyes opened in stunned disbelief to look into Jon's. He was bending towards the bed. His shirt was soaked through, clinging to his skin and he had brought in with him the cool fresh smell of rain. He opened his mouth to speak, the words drowned out by the ferocity of the storm, the brilliance of the lightning jagging across the sky making Sophy scream out in terror and release her pillow to fling herself against him, burying her face in his shoulder.

She felt him shake and for a moment thought he was laughing at her but then she felt his hand on her hair, his voice roughly concerned in her ear, as his arms came round her, and his voice soothed her fear.

'I'll go and close the curtains.'

She didn't want to let him go but suddenly all that had happened reminded her that she had no right to be in his arms ... no place within their security and so she withdrew from him, and watched him walk across the floor.

The curtains were thick, old-fashioned ones, and instantly blotted out the storm, together with what little daylight there was. In the gloom she could barely make out Jon's outline, until he switched on the bedside lamp.

'That's some storm out there,' he told her wryly. 'I'm soaked ... I'll have to take this off.' He stripped off his shirt, dropping it into the laundry basket, opening his wardrobe to get another; all simple automatic movements and yet ones that moved her to great joy and pain. He didn't put the shirt on though, pausing to turn and look across the room at her.

'Sophy, why wouldn't you let me talk to you?'

His voice was quiet, and if she hadn't known better she might have said it was quite definitely edged with pain.

She could feel the tight knot returning to her chest and couldn't speak, simply shaking her head. She knew he was coming towards her and that she should get off his bed and move away but something told her that her legs simply would not allow her to stand. As he reached her he stretched out his hand, and gently tugged away the shirt she had been clinging to.

A hot wave of colour flooded her skin as Sophy found herself unable to free herself from his gaze. He had taken off his glasses—to dry them, she supposed, and had not put them back, so that she could quite clearly see the wry amusement darkening his eyes to indigo blue.

'What's this?'

He said it softly, watching her like a hunter stalking his prey ... seeing far too much for someone who was supposed to be so short-sighted.

'I was cold.'

She saw his eyebrows lift with pardonable mockery, shock jolting through her body as he said softly. 'How disappointing ... I was hoping it was a love-object substitute ...' he sat down beside her and concluded silkily, 'and that that love-object was me.'

How could he do this to her? Her fingers curled into her palms, not even the dying sound of the storm having the power to frighten her now.

'Why are you saying these things to me?' she demanded huskily. 'Isn't Lillian enough for you?'

His prompt 'No,' stunned her. She could only stare silently up at him, her mouth slightly open. All humour had gone from his eyes now and in fact they were almost frightingly grim.

'I could shake you, Sophy, for being so stupid,' he told her bitingly. 'How on earth could you be so easily deceived?'

'Deceived?'

'I don't care what Lillian might have told you.' He reached out and cupped her face. 'Sophy, Lillian and I were never lovers. Oh, I know what she told you,' he continued before she could speak, 'but only because Mary-Beth told me. I had no idea that Lillian had——' He broke off, his mouth curling in bitter derision. 'That woman astounds me, astounds and frightens ...'

'Jon ...'

'No ... listen to me. Let me tell you the full story,' he paused and when she made no move to speak he started softly, 'I told you that I met Lillian when I went to Nassau but what I didn't tell you was that she seemed to develop what, for lack of a better description, I can only describe as some sort of fixation about me.' He grimaced faintly. 'It got so bad that I was actually having to find ways to avoid her. When she first invited me to use her apartment and pool I had no idea. In the end I had to appeal to Mary-Beth for help and it was then that I discovered that Lillian has a history of these almost violent fixations. It's a sad story in a way. In many respects she's absolutely brilliant ... perhaps almost too much so. Apparently she had some sort of breakdown just after she left university but she's very good at her job and Harry, who's a bit of a softie in many ways, took her on to his staff after he heard about her history of mental problems from his predecessor. Workwise he has no criticism of her at all but emotionally, she doesn't seem to have any conception of reality or self-control.

'When he told me all this I was glad that I was leaving Nassau so soon—and not only for that reason,' he added cryptically. 'I got the shock of my life when I walked into that hotel in London and found her waiting for me there in the foyer. Apparently Harry had had to ring Nassau and he had spoken to her on the telephone—about some problems she was having with her work. She asked him about me and without thinking he mentioned that I was going to London to do some work for Lexicons, which happens to be a company that Nassau deal with.' He shrugged tiredly.

'Harry admits now that that was a mistake, but as he says, it never even crossed his mind that Lillian would ring Lexicons, pretending to be my wife and find out from them which hotel they had booked me into and when I could be expected there.' He saw Sophy's expression and smiled harshly, 'She was quite proud of what she did, believe me. For me it was like the start of a nightmare. Every time I tried to persuade her to go back to Nassau she started threatening to destroy herself. Finally I managed to persuade her to let me ring Harry and he came down to London straight away to talk to her.

'The plan was that Harry would see her safely on to a plane to go home and that she would be met at the other end but somehow it backfired and she managed to give Harry the slip.

'He rang me yesterday morning to warn me. That was why I went out to see him so that we could try and work out what on earth she was going to do. The last thing I expected was that she would turn up here.

'Lillian is an extremely mentally disturbed young woman, Sophy,' he said quietly. 'If I give you my word that she and I have never been lovers and that I would never want her as my lover, would you believe me?'

'Where is she now?' Her throat was dry with tension.

'With Harry and Mary-Beth. I managed to persuade her to drive me over there yesterday afternoon. I thought you were angry with me because I hadn't told you what was happening. I should have done but our own relationship seemed too tenuous . . . so fragile that I felt I couldn't risk destroying it by burdening you with problems that weren't really yours. Especially after the shock of Chris's attack.'

'She said you loved her . . .' Her voice was cracked and uneven. 'She said you wanted to divorce me.'

'She's a very sick person, Sophy, so totally out of touch with reality that I'm afraid she'll never be wholly sane again. Believe me, I did nothing . . . nothing to encourage her in her fantasies.' He smiled rather grimly. 'There was only one woman on my mind whilst I was in Nassau and that was you. Do you believe me?'

'Yes.' She said it huskily and knew that it was true. Her heart somersaulted as he lifted her hand to his mouth and pressed his lips to her palm, caressing it softly with his tongue.

'How did you know what Lillian had said to me?'

'Mary-Beth told me. She also told me something else.' Sophy tensed and looked at him, remembering her own admission to Mary-Beth that she loved him.

'She said you were frightened of thunder storms,' Jon told her softly, 'and that she'd told you to bury your head under a pillow. I'm glad you chose my pillow, Sophy.'

She could feel the heat coming off his skin, and being in his arms was like coming home to safety having known great pain and fear. His mouth touched hers, lightly, questioningly and she clung to him, abandoning all pride as she was swamped by her own shattering response to him.

She could feel his heart thudding erratically against her, his mouth hot and urgent as it moved over her own. She wanted him to go on kissing her for ever, but already he was releasing her, putting a distance between them.

'I still haven't been entirely honest with you.'

She thought for a moment her heart-beat had stopped. He smiled gravely at her and said quietly,

'When I asked you to marry me I had no intention of it ever being merely a convenient arrangement, devoid of love and physical contact.'

'You hadn't?'

He shook his head, said 'No,' and then laughed at her expression. 'I begin to think you're the one who needs glasses, Mrs Philips,' he teased her softly, 'otherwise you'd surely have seen that I'd been lusting after you ever since you came to work for me. From the very first time we met in fact.'

She stared at him in disbelief, stammering, 'But . . . but I thought——'

'That I was a sexless, vague, confirmed bachelor, more interested in computers, than human beings,' he said wryly, 'Oh yes, I do realise that and I had been cursing my far too effective armour plating for quite some considerable time. It was the look on your face when you heard David saying that Louise had wanted to get into bed with me that finally gave me hope.'

'What sort of look?' Sophy asked him suspiciously.

His smile was both innocent and tantalising. 'Oh, the sort that said you were looking at me as a man instead of simply your lame dog boss.'

Sophy shook her head. 'But why pretend to be something you weren't, Jon? Why pretend to be so sexless and . . . dull?'

He hesitated for a moment and then said slowly, 'I know this will make me sound unattractively vain but when I first went up to Cambridge, like many another before me I wanted to have a good time. My father was comfortably off . . . those were the days when teenagers didn't have to worry too much about getting a job . . . when, in fact, our generation thought it was the hub of the whole world. It was my first real time away from home, I had a generous allowance and a small sports car my father had bought me when I passed my 'A' levels. I wasn't short of congenial feminine company. In short I lived a life of hedonistic pleasure rather than scholarly concentration. That all came to an abrupt end just after my third term. My tutors started complaining about the standard of my work ... that sobered me up quite a bit, until then I'd never really had to work, you could say that it had all come too easily to me. Then a friend of mine was sent down—drug trafficking; a girl I'd gone out with died—all alone in a filthy squat with her arm all bloated out with septic poisoning from using a dirty needle—she was mainlining on heroin. I had to identify her. It all brought me down to reality.

'When term resumed after the Christmas recess I decided I was going to turn over a new leaf. I'd talked to my brother—Hugh was eight years older than me, already married then, but still enough in touch with his own youth to listen sympathetically to me—but it seemed that my friends or at least some of them didn't want me to change. Then I had to start wearing glasses. I discovered quite quickly that people who didn't know me reacted differently to me ... and so gradually I evolved a form of disguise and somehow it stuck with me. There was nothing to make me want to abandon it, until I met you and even then it seemed I wasn't going to be able to reveal myself to you in my true colours, so to speak.'

Sophy looked questioningly at him and he said drolly,

'Ah well, you see I had observed how you reacted to me ... and how you reacted to any male who was even just slightly aggressively masculine and I didn't want to frighten you off. You felt safe with me, that much was obvious and because of that I could get closer to you. Some disguises are used for protection,' he told her, 'some for hunting ...' He laughed at her expression. 'Ah yes, my poor little love, I'm afraid you ...'

She didn't let him finish, flushing suddenly as she remembered his bland and extremely irritating indifference to her timid sexual overtures in the early days of their marriage ... an indifference which she had naïvely thought sprang from unawareness.

'You knew ...' she accused.

'Knew what?' He was smiling dulcetly at her.

She swallowed, and said huskily, 'That I wanted you.'

After the way you looked at me when I came back from Nassau I hoped you might,' he agreed tenderly, 'but I had to be sure it wasn't merely that I was a challenge to you, Sophy. I had gambled too heavily for that. You see,' he told her quietly, 'as I soon discovered well before I married you, what I once thought was merely lust turned out to be love and that love hasn't diminished for knowing you ... quite the contrary. *That* is what I have been trying to talk to you about, Sophy.' He touched her face lightly with his fingers and she trembled wildly, hardly daring to look at him. 'We have been lovers, and you have given yourself to me physically with a generosity that no one else has ever matched or ever could, but have you given yourself to me emotionally, Sophy? *Can* you give yourself to me emotionally or is it still Benson, despite all that he has done to you?'

'Chris?' Sophy stared at him. 'I never loved Chris. Not really, not like . . .'

'Not like?' His voice was placid, belying the expression in his eyes. It made her heart race and suspended her breath until she realised he was still waiting impatiently for her response.

'Not like I love you,' she told him.

He expelled his breath on a harsh sigh and said roughly, 'God, Sophy, you don't know how you've tormented me.'

She smiled at him, going willingly into his arms as he dragged her against him. 'Oh, I think I've a fair idea,' she told him demurely, 'after all you've done your own fair share of tormenting.'

From the shelter of his arms, she looked up at him, watching the way his eyebrows rose in query.

'All that parading around practically nude,' she elucidated for him, 'making me want you, making me love you . . .' She looked up at him again and smiled, 'and probably damn well making me pregnant into the bargain.'

'Have I done?' He looked smugly and irritatingly malely pleased at the prospect.

'I don't know,' she admitted, 'but, Jon . . .' she protested as he turned round with her still in his arms and rolled her onto the bed, following her there, and pinning her down with the superior weight of his body.

'Jon, what are you doing?' she demanded.

He was grinning at her and her heart turned over inside her as she read the purpose in his eyes and he told her softly, 'It would certainly be one

sure fire way of keeping you tied to me. Besides . . .'
He paused to kiss her, smothering her mumbled
protest until she was forced to give up and respond
to him.

'Besides . . . what?' she asked breathlessly when
at last he had released her.

'I love loving you so much,' he told her simply.
'No woman has ever meant to me what you do,
Sophy, or ever will. I could have wept when you
told me that you weren't fully a woman. I could
have killed Benson for what he had done to you.
You were too inexperienced to even realise what
he *had* done. How he had pushed his own
inadequacies off on to you.'

'*You* made me a woman, Jon,' she told him
huskily, feeling his body tense against her and
thrilling to the vibrant masculinity of it. Only one
thing still troubled her, creasing her forehead as
she said hesitantly, 'Jon, just now when I said I
might be pregnant you seemed pleased but you
threatened to put the children into care. You . . .'

'I gambled that their supposed plight would
push you into marrying me far faster than any
amount of reasoned argument,' he admitted wryly,
'but believe me I would never have done it.
They're my brother's children, Sophy, and I love
them very much, just as I shall love our own very
much . . . but never quite as much as I love you.'

Beneath him her body quivered and she reached
up to wrap her arms round him, her voice
breaking slightly as she murmured, 'Make love to
me please, Jon. Show me that this isn't all some
impossible dream.'

'No dream but reality,' he whispered against her
mouth. 'The reality of our love.'

Harlequin Presents

Coming Next Month

Available in December wherever paperback books are sold, or through Harlequin Reader Service:

In the U.S.
P.O. Box 1397
Buffalo, N.Y.
14240-1397

In Canada
P.O. Box 603
Fort Erie, Ontario
L2A 9Z9

Six exciting series
for you every month...
from Harlequin

Harlequin Romance·
The series that started it all

Tender, captivating and heartwarming...
love stories that sweep you off to faraway places
and delight you with the magic of love.

◆

Harlequin Presents·
Powerful contemporary love
stories...as individual as the
women who read them

The No. 1 romance series...
exciting love stories for you, the woman of today...
a rare blend of passion and dramatic realism.

◆

Harlequin Superromance®
It's more than romance...
it's Harlequin Superromance

A sophisticated, contemporary romance-fiction
series, providing you with a longer,
more involving read...a richer mix of complex plots,
realism and adventure.

Harlequin
American Romance™
Harlequin celebrates the American woman...

...by offering you romance stories written about American women, by American women for American women. This series offers you contemporary romances uniquely North American in flavor and appeal.

◆

Harlequin Temptation...
Passionate stories for today's woman

An exciting series of sensual, mature stories of love...dilemmas, choices, resolutions... all contemporary issues dealt with in a true-to-life fashion by some of your favorite authors.

◆

Harlequin Intrigue
Because romance can be quite an adventure

Harlequin Intrigue, an innovative series that blends the romance you expect... with the unexpected. Each story has an added element of intrigue that provides a new twist to the Harlequin tradition of romance excellence.

Harlequin Books·

PROD-A-2

Take 4 novels and a surprise gift FREE